D0044629

OPERATION
FINAL NOTICE

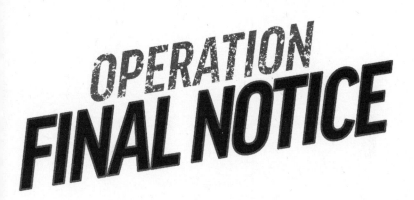

MATTHEW LANDIS

DIAL BOOKS FOR YOUNG READERS

Dial Books for Young Readers
An imprint of Penguin Random House LLC, New York

First published in the United States of America by Dial Books for Young Readers,
an imprint of Penguin Random House LLC, 2022

Copyright © 2022 by Matthew Landis

Dial & colophon are registered trademarks of Penguin Random House LLC.
The Penguin colophon is a registered trademark of Penguin Books Limited.

Visit us online at penguinrandomhouse.com.

Library of Congress Cataloging-in-Publication Data is available.
Manufactured in Canada
ISBN 9780593109755

1 3 5 7 9 10 8 6 4 2

FRI

Design by Cerise Steel
Text set in Eureka Pro

TO MUSIC AND LEARNING SUPPORT TEACHERS.
YOU ARE SUPERHEROES.

"TO LIVE IS NOT ENOUGH; WE MUST TAKE PART."
—PABLO CASALS

1

THE INVITATION

JO

PAPI lays the envelope next to my dinner plate. I put my fork down and stare at it.

I've been waiting three months for it. We mailed the application back in August, just before I started seventh grade.

"It won't open itself," Mami says.

Papi smiles. His large black eyes sparkle. "Go on, mijita."

I turn the envelope over and slowly pry it open. I'm worried about tearing it—like any mistake now could change what's inside.

Mami scoots her chair next to mine at our small kitchen table. She smells like bleach and lavender from a day spent cleaning houses with Señora Reyes. "You can always apply next year," she says. "Si sabes, verdad?"

"I know."

But I don't want to apply next year—I want to *be* there next year.

I break the seal and pull out the letter. Mami whispers a prayer to La Virgencita. Papi leans forward, his elbows on the table. There is no sound in the apartment except for my pounding heart.

I unfold the piece of paper and read the typed note.

Dear Ms. Josefina Ramos,

We are pleased to invite you for an audition . . .

I don't read the rest.

Instead, I laugh—and get smothered in a family hug.

Maple Hill Conservatory, here I come.

2

CHEESE IS IN MY FUTURE

RONNY

I'M dreaming about cheese when Bianca wakes me up with her weird sleep talking.

"Dragonfly," she says.

I'm real confused because where am I? I sit up and bang my head on the ceiling because these rooms are super small and I been sharing a bunkbed with my fifth-grade sister for two years now.

"Dragonfly," she says again.

"No dragonflies in here." The little clock on our desk says 5:38 so I get off the top bunk to get dressed for school and check on Bianca. Her hair is all over her whole face like a brown blanket. "Are you okay?"

She says something but she's sleeping again in a couple seconds. I pull the covers up and she has like a hundred animal books in all these stacks on the floor so it's hard to not knock them all over and wake her up.

I'm getting my socks on and see a bedroom light in one of the townhome windows right across the street. It's way up high because the garages there are on the bottom and I remember always going up a ton of steps to get to my room which is funny because now our apartment has zero steps and is really tiny. Probably the kid who lives in my old room doesn't have to share a bunkbed with his little sister and deal with her weird dreams.

I go to the kitchen and there's my mom in her blue nurse clothes for work. She's eating breakfast and doing her favorite thing which is reading one of the papers from the giant blue folder of bills.

"Hey bud," she says. "How'd you sleep?"

"Good."

"Any dreams?"

"Cheese."

"Again?"

"Yeah, I know."

"Not turkey?"

"Ha come on," I say because last week she got this big Thanksgiving food box thing at the grocery store with the good stuff. She made this giant turkey and I ate so much but there was more turkey left so we had to keep eating it for dinner. "No, it was cheese."

"Hmm," she says. She always sits up real straight when she does her bills, like she's in the army or something. Her hair used to be long like Bianca's until she cut it shorter than mine last year. "You do like cheese."

"Probably it's a sign. Like cheese is in my future."

"Or maybe it was my amazing dinner last night, which included cheese."

"Yeah, probably it was both."

I eat cereal and she's staring at this bill that says *FINAL NOTICE* in big red letters. I see her do bills every morning but I never seen her face get real serious like this. Now she's looking under the table at my jeans and grabbing the bottoms.

"Are those pants too small?"

"Come on, they're fine."

"You're getting taller."

"Yeah, I'm a seventh-grade giant," I say which is zero true because I'm barely taller than my friend Jo Ramos and she's a girl.

"They look small."

"Mom, come on."

"You're growing so fast."

She makes this weird face like something hurts and now she's looking at the FINAL NOTICE bill again. It's real quiet and I can hear my dad doing his back exercises in him and my mom's room. It stinks because they hurt him but the doctor said it's the only way to get better after the surgery.

"Probably you should get Bianca's brain checked out," I say.

"What?"

"She talks about bugs in her sleep."

"I can't tell if you're serious."

"Mom, I'm serious," I say but I'm sort of laughing.

"It's always so hard to tell."

"She could have a condition. Probably you should scan her head with one of those machines at your work."

She's laughing too. "So now you're a doctor?"

"I mean there's something happening up in her brain cage you should get checked."

She's pushing her plate across to me. "Eat some toast."

We eat toast and now the people above us are stomping around their kitchen. Bianca gets up and is banging around the bathroom.

"I'm gonna go play games on my laptop," I say.

"Maybe I should have them scan *your* brain."

"Ha yeah and ask about the cheese dreams."

"You need to eat some fruit."

"No, I'm good," I say. "I have cheese in my future."

I go into the living room and pretend to play games but really I'm googling FINAL NOTICE. It says *a final letter or other communication sent to somebody by a creditor warning that if payment is not made on a specific date, legal action will be taken.*

Now I'm looking up *creditor* and it says *a person or company to whom money is owed.*

My breakfast feels like slushy snow in my stomach because I've seen *legal action* before. It was on that big orange sticker they put on our townhouse window right by the front door and like a week later we were moving into this super small apartment.

Jo knocks on the door and my mom is hugging me. "Have a good day, buddy. Love ya."

"Yeah," I say, and she's looking at the FINAL NOTICE bill again all serious.

3

THE SECRET

JO

I walk down the Apartment's sidewalk with Ronny. I'm excited—and nervous. I didn't tell him I applied to Maple Hill. I wanted to wait until I actually got the invitation.

And Esther—I need to tell her too.

I *have* to do it soon.

Today?

"I think it was cheddar," Ronny says. He fixes his snow hat and pushes a dark clump of hair out of his eyes. "Like it was all shredded."

"What color was it?" I ask.

"Orange. Or the yellow kind."

We climb onto the school bus. I sit with my cello, and Ronny plops down in front of me with my backpack. Inside is my music folder.

Inside *that* is The Secret.

I say, "You were swimming in it?"

"Maybe I was drowning."

"Was it a pool?"

"Probably it was an ocean." He puts his chin on the seat back and stares at me. "It's gotta mean something. People just don't have cheese dreams for no reason."

Our bus driver shuts the door and we lurch forward. Ronny draws circles on the foggy window with a finger. Should I tell him now?

No—the ride is too short. So at lunch, then.

But Mason and Esther will be there.

After school?

We drive the long loop around the Apartments to the exit. The light turns yellow, and the driver slams on the brakes. My book bag flies into the aisle and bursts open.

I see my music folder on the ground, wide-open. The envelope sticks out of the left pocket.

"Have you ever heard of final notice?" Ronny asks me. He tucks the envelope back in the pocket and puts everything in my book bag. "Like on a bill in the mail."

How did he not see it?

I say, "I don't know."

"Man, I really need to see that bill again."

Today—I will tell him today. On the way to lunch, when it's just me and him walking. I *have* to. He needs to know.

It changes things—for both of us.

At school, we walk to the string closet to drop off my cello. Mr. Newsum, the orchestra director, sits at his desk pouring hot water into a fancy glass container. He examines the dark droplets falling to the bottom, nodding to himself. From the pocket of his big winter sweater, he pulls out a little sand timer and sets it on the desk.

"Ronny," he says. "Jo-Jo Ma. How goes it?"

I say, "Good."

"More cheese dreams," Ronny says.

"Swiss?"

"Oceans of cheddar," Ronny says. "Probably I should see a brain doctor."

Mr. Newsum folds his hands behind his head and sticks his legs out. He isn't that tall, but it seems like it because he's always lounging. Like most of the teachers at Kennesaw, he's white. "I had a weird dream last night too. I was in the middle of the school gym with hundreds of folding chairs lying on the ground."

"Ha," Ronny says. "That sounds like a nightmare."

"What happened?" I ask.

"I picked them all up and arranged the place into an auditorium." Mr. Newsum shrugs and tucks some curly dark hair behind his ear. "Seemed like a good idea. And then I started singing the *happy birthday* song. This is where it gets weird."

"Oh man it's just getting weird," Ronny says.

"Mrs. Fastbender, our *fearless* school leader, walks in with a birthday cake. She holds it out in front of me, to blow out—and then shoves the whole thing in my face."

Ronny laughs—hard. I say, "That *is* weird."

"Indeed." Mr. Newsum checks his coffee timer and then takes a sip. "So: Jo. Get anything in the mail over the weekend?"

I freeze.

"Oh man, right in your face," Ronny says. "That definitely means something."

I look at Ronny, and then shake my head.

"You should've gotten it," Mr. Newsum says. "They usually mail them out the week of Thanksgiving."

"I think something embarrassing is going to happen to you soon," Ronny says to Mr. Newsum. "And you should definitely stay away from cake for a while. Like if there is a party happening, you should go as far away as you can. Probably take a week off of work."

Ronny's never-ending joke cycle can be very helpful sometimes—it gives me time to think.

"We should get breakfast," I tell Ronny. "Before the eighth graders take all the hash browns. Let's go."

I wave to Mr. Newsum and walk out. I feel sick.

I can't wait any longer—he needs to know.

We get in line for breakfast. I say, "Ronny."

"Present."

"Remember when I went to that orchestra camp last summer?"

"Yeah." His voice sounds far away. He points to a sign near the food trays.

WE ARE OUT OF CHEESE.

"Is this a dream?" he whispers.

I laugh. "Wow."

"*WE ARE OUT OF CHEESE!*" he yells.

The cafeteria ladies frown at him.

We get our food, and then go to the register. Ronny and I give the lady our student numbers, and she rings us up even though we don't have to pay for breakfast or lunch—most kids who live in the Apartments don't.

"My brain should be studied," he tells her. "I had a dream this was gonna happen."

"Please don't yell like that again," she says, and waves for the next student in line.

We sit at the end of a long lunch table. Ronny eats his hash brown in two bites. "Probably there's a milk situation happening. Like the cows forgot how to do it."

"Ronny—"

"Or like all the cheese workers got sick or something—"

"*Ronny!*"

He takes a big bite of bagel—his cheeks are packed with food. "*Wha?*"

"I might be leaving next year."

4

JO IS MAYBE LEAVING NEXT YEAR

RONNY

"LEAINGWAH?" I say.

"What?"

I swallow but everything gets stuck and now I'm choking on sausage and bagel with no cheese. Jo is whacking me on the back and I'm coughing it all up on the wrapper.

"Are you okay?" she says.

I cough a bunch more. "Oh man, probably you're a hero."

She's staring at me all weird and playing with her giant black braid. "I'm sorry—I should've told you that I applied to Maple Hill."

"It's okay," I say real quick and now something weird and not bagel-choking related is happening in my gut. It's really cold and hurts like two snowmen are punching each other. *"So where are you going?"*

Jo gets her music folder and is showing me this fancy pamphlet thing that says *Maple Hill Conservatory: Premier Music School* in swirly letters. I look through it and there's kids playing instruments outside and then on a stage and wow in a big auditorium that's way nicer than ours. Pretty much every place you can think of they're playing instruments.

"This is where you did the cello camp thing," I say.

She's nodding and now she's showing me this letter that says *Dear Ms. Josefina Ramos. We are pleased to invite you for an audition with the Maple Hill String Faculty* blah blah blah I don't want to read the rest. I give it back and man my barfed-up bagel looks pretty gross on the wrapper so I'm crumpling it all up. Jo gives me half of hers and I'm eating it but I'm not really hungry anymore.

"Mr. Newsum has a friend who works there," she says. "He said I should apply because there's not much more he can teach me. Private teachers are too expensive."

"Yeah and you want to be the next Carlos Prieto," I say, because he's this big famous cello guy on a poster in her room. There's one of Yo-Yo Ma too and Jo says they're like the LeBron James and Michael Jordan of cello. "You want to play cello all the time and be like him."

Jo is nodding. "I'll still go to the regular classes, but more of the school day will be cello—with special teachers. They can even pay for my tuition too."

"Whoa that's good."

"But it's not for sure yet," she says real quiet. "I have an audition in January—in front of all the string teachers. Then they'll decide to let me in or not."

"Yeah but you're gonna get in."

Man she's pulling hard on that braid. "I don't like . . . solos."

"Yeah but come on," I say, but now I'm thinking about all the orchestra stuff I been to and has she ever done a solo at one of those? Esther has done a bunch but Jo is way better than her. "I mean you play like eight hours a day. You're gonna get in."

The big giant guidance counselor Mr. Killroy starts letting kids go to first period. "I'm sorry I didn't tell you," Jo says.

"Yeah but it's okay. I mean you saved me from choking on a bagel."

She's sort of laughing and snowmen are like body slamming each other in my stomach and now I'm going to first period where I do zero paying attention.

5

THE OTHER SECRET

JO

AFTER school, I get to the stage early for string ensemble rehearsal. Just me.

My fingers find each note perfectly because I've played this opening every day for two years—Schumann's *Three Fantasy Pieces*. I *should* warm up with scales, or Popper's etudes to stretch my hands. But this piece is so beautiful that it has to be played every day.

I hear footsteps and stop.

"I made brownies," Esther says. She puts her cello down and hands me a ziplock bag. "For the bake sale. Dark chocolate. This is the test batch."

I take a bite. Warm, fudgy cake swirls in my mouth. "This is really good."

She leans close to me. "Better than Samantha's chocolate chip cookies, right?"

"Those were good too."

"Yes." Esther rolls her eyes. "But the chocolate chip cookie is over. *Everyone* brings those. It's time to move on to the brownie."

She tunes her cello and runs through a C major scale. Her brownish-red hair sweeps across her freckled face, and soon she'll be covered in sweat. Even during warm-ups, Esther plays like she's wrestling a bear—that's why she wears gym clothes to rehearsal. Mr. Newsum tried to correct her technique last year, but gave up because she never seemed to get tired.

I say, "I have to tell you something."

She puts her bow down. "Is this about me using your rosin? Because it's only a little bit each time."

"No—"

"I guess it does add up because I use it almost every day—"

"Jo-Jo Ma." Mr. Newsum walks over to us. He salutes Esther, and then narrows his eyes at me. "*Well?*"

Esther stares at me. This feels easier than Ronny finding out—leaving won't change that much for her. She'll probably become first chair.

I say, "I got the letter."

"What letter?" Esther asks.

A smile takes over my face. "An invitation to audition at Maple Hill."

"*What?*" She blinks very fast. "Oh my gosh."

Mr. Newsum high-fives me. "When's the audition?"

I feel a beehive stir in my stomach. "January fourth."

"*Maple Hill,*" Esther whispers. She hugs the neck of her cello. "You're leaving."

"I should've told you before," I say. Is she mad? "I'm sorry—I wanted to wait until I knew for sure."

"No. It's *amazing*." She tightens the hairs on her bow. "What do they want you to play?"

I take the invitation out and read from the list. "Major scales in twelve keys."

"You could do that without practicing," Esther says.

"A Kummer melody or similar etude to show technique."

"Your Popper Number One will blow their argyle socks right off," Mr. Newsum says.

I say, "And two contrasting movements of any period piece. Bach suites are highly encouraged."

"Hmmm." Mr. Newsum taps a finger on his coffee mug. "The preludes in G and D Minor should satisfy their clipboards. You put in a lot of hours on them this summer."

My finger finds the large dent on the top of the cello. Nobody knows how it got there—not even Ronny.

That's my *other* secret.

The one that might keep me out of Maple Hill.

I say, "I don't like solos."

"*Really?*" Mr. Newsum drops his jaw and pretends to be surprised. "I had *absolutely* no idea."

I study him. "You *know*?"

"Two years of private lessons, and not one time were you 'available' for our Friday night Coffee House gigs. Or that quartet invitation from the high school string teacher." He smirks. "And then there was the *mysterious* misplacing of the talent show sign-up forms. Tell me: How does a person as organized as *Jo Ramos* keep losing just that one handout?"

Esther looks around the neck of her cello at me. "Is that why you wouldn't play in the entryway last year? When we took turns doing welcome music for parents at the spring concert?"

That was right after The Incident in Mexico that put the first dent on my cello. "I know—it's weird," I say.

"It's not . . . weird." Esther lowers her voice. "But the cello is a *solo* instrument. And you're so good."

If I'm in my room—alone. Or onstage with the rest of the ensemble. But I get nervous even during private lessons with Mr. Newsum if he's not working through the piece with me on his cello.

"Wait—*wait*," Mr. Newsum says. He holds up a finger. "Oh, this is good. This is timely."

He runs over to his music stand and comes back with a green flyer. "Mrs. Vargas is taking her select choir over to the Manor, the senior citizen home down the hill. They go every year to cheer up the old folks with some caroling. I think they would LOVE a cello performance at the back end. What say you?"

I blink. "You want me to play—you want me to do a solo."

"Indeed."

"For all those people." The beehive buzzes in my stomach. "This Friday."

He nods. "The only way to *do something* is to *do something*. Remember third position? You couldn't do that—until you played it a hundred times."

"Third position," Esther whispers. "It's so scary up there."

"Fear not the unknown," Mr. Newsum says. "I'm gonna email you some breathing exercises to try this week, really good stuff that calms your nerves." He conducts the air in a slow four count, and then points to me at the end of the imaginary measure. "So, Jo: Do you accept this challenge?"

6

MS. Q IS AWESOME

RONNY

"HEY look at this," Bri says to me in fourth period.

"What?" I say because I'm still googling the crap out of *FINAL NOTICE* stuff. Probably I need the actual bill thing but when I got home from school yesterday it wasn't there. Maybe there's another pile in her room for like the super extra scary bills and I should look there today.

"Come on, look," Bri says.

"Okay."

It's just a couple of us in Ms. Q's seventh-grade reading class. We have her for English too right before this because she's our Learning Support teacher which basically means our brains learn slower and we need extra help. Plus I have this thing called ADHD which means it's hard to focus but Ms. Q says that's not an excuse to do whatever I want.

"Watch."

"I'm watching," I say and she's showing me a video on her phone. It's her holding a big white cat that's *meowing* sounds but instead of the *meow* it's a girl singing.

"That's Beyoncé," Bri says.

"Your cat?"

"No, the song."

"Oh right."

"Taylor Swift loves Beyoncé."

"What?"

"My cat," she says. "Taylor Swift."

"Ha right."

We keep watching and I hear Ms. Q in the hallway reading test questions to Julius. At the front table Larissa is doing this big giant review thing Mr. Carrow made for our social studies test on the Constitution and I'm supposed to be doing it too. If Ms. Q comes in we're gonna get a lot of big nose-exhales from her because basically fourth period is for finishing late work in other classes.

"You think she's really singing?" Bri says.

"Probably not."

"Look at her mouth. She's right with the words."

"I don't know if cats can do that."

Bri is singing along with the video now. "It would be cool if she could."

"Yeah but it would also be pretty scary because a singing cat? And then the scientists would take it away from you to study probably—"

"How's the Constitution coming?" Ms. Q says.

Bri puts her phone away real quick and we both pretend to be working on our laptops.

"Good," I say.

Ms. Q comes over and looks at our screens from way up in her tall person view. She's got blond hair and is real pale and is always folding her long arms like a praying mantis. "Looks like . . . you've done nothing."

"I did some," I say.

"Not enough."

"Sorry," Bri says.

Ms. Q pushes out a big nose-exhale. "Let's work by ourselves. I'll check in with you in five."

I go back to my table and stare at the diagram of *U.S. Government Checks and Balances*. Mr. Carrow loves the Constitution so he gives us a ton of charts that are supposed to be cool but are really just confusing. I blur my eyes and the whole thing goes into a blob and then I see a shape like in one of those hidden picture things. It's a dollar sign at first but then it's a cello. I'm blinking real fast but it's still there and now the snowmen are doing battle again in my stomach.

"How's it going?" Ms. Q says.

"Good."

She's looking over my questions. "Ronny."

"Present."

"You answered two of them."

"Yeah."

"There are five."

"Affirmative."

She's rolling up her sleeves and sitting next to me. Most

teachers look fancy at work but Ms. Q says she teaches better when she feels better and that means ponytails and jeans and school T-shirts for sports she never coached. Today it says *Kennesaw Track and Field.* "That's not correct."

"Yeah," I say. "Ha did you know Mr. Carrow named his son Washington? Like after George Washington, come on isn't that weird?"

"Mr. Carrow is an interesting person."

"Yeah but not as weird as Mr. Newsum. He's having these cake nightmares—"

"Ronny."

"Yup."

"The review questions were due before Thanksgiving break. And then you said you'd do them during the break." More big sighs are coming from Ms. Q. "And here we are."

"Yeah, I was really busy giving thanks."

Julius laughs but Ms. Q is just staring at me pretty hard. She never gets mad at us but sometimes she gets really annoyed and I'm pretty sure that's right now.

"Okay but for real," I say. "Bri has a cat that can maybe sing Beyoncé so focusing is hard right now. And I almost died on a bagel sandwich yesterday because of a cheese outage going on in this place."

"Are you sick?" Ms. Q says.

They're all laughing now except Ms. Q and I'm looking right at her and the words fly out before I can stop them.

"Ha yeah I'm sick of this class."

Julius goes *oooooo* and Larissa covers her mouth and oh man I'm feeling sweaty. Kids are walking by in the halls and Ms. Q hasn't blinked in like forever.

"Stay," she says to me. "The rest of you: Head to your specials. Have a great day."

Everybody leaves but I don't go to art and now she's eating peanut butter crackers at her desk.

"Are you gonna email my mom?" I say.

"Negative."

"Oh man good," I say because Ms. Q is awesome and what was I even doing? Getting in trouble now would be like ten more FINAL NOTICE bills to my mom. "That was really bad I'm sorry."

"I forgive you." She's chugging water from this big tall bottle she always uses. "Tell me about almost dying on a bagel sandwich."

"Ha yeah so I was choking on a bagel and Jo hit me on the back and I barfed in front of her. Probably some got on her like you know how that happens when you barf?"

"I get the picture. Good thing she was there."

"Yeah but she made me choke on the bagel," I say and it's like the angry snowmen in my gut are chucking each other up into my throat.

"How did she—?"

"She's leaving," I say real loud. "She's going to a cello school next year if she does good on her audition which, come on, she's gonna do amazing because she's the next Carlos Prieto."

"Who's that?"

"The greatest Mexican cello player of all time. She's gonna be more famous than him."

"I did hear Mr. Newsum say something about her potential." Ms. Q comes over and sits by me now. "Ronny: I'm sorry. That stinks. But: You're neighbors. You'll still hang out after school."

"Probably she'll have new cello friends."

"It will be different, and you'll miss her. But she's not moving to Canada." Ms. Q is writing me a pass now to art. "And you'll hang out with other friends—like Mason. He still lives close to you."

"Yeah maybe," I say but Mason and I don't really hang out like we used to before they put that big orange sticker on our townhouse with the *legal action* stuff. "Hey, can you go to jail if you don't pay money back to people?"

"What?"

"Like if you borrow money to buy a house or something but you can't pay it back."

"No, you won't go to jail," Ms. Q says. "Usually the bank takes it back."

Yeah and puts big orange stickers on it so the whole neighborhood knows. "But like after that can they get you in legal action trouble?"

"I don't think so." She's looking at me real weird. "Ronny: What's up?"

But her room phone is ringing and now I'm going to art and oh man I need to find my mom's secret bill folder.

My dad's back surgery stuff? That was crazy expensive.

Bianca's braces? I mean she's annoying but I don't want her to have messed-up teeth.

What part of us is *legal action* gonna take next?

7

ESTAS MANOS

JO

"AND I told Tía Rosa," Mami tells me at dinner. " 'That Josefina!' she said."

I push my food around. Ronny didn't come over today—I think he's avoiding me. I knew I should have told him about Maple Hill sooner.

But would it have mattered? I still might be leaving.

Might be.

" 'That Josefina!' Tía Rosa said. 'She will be playing all over the world one day.' "

I say, "I didn't get accepted yet."

Papi catches my eye and winks. "Maria," he says to my mom, "maybe we should wait to tell everyone until after the audition."

"Audition—please." Mami shakes her head. A few strands of black hair come out of her work bun. "She's a natural. Mr. Newsum said so."

"You know I have . . . problems, with solos," I say. I point to the permission slip on the counter. "That's why he invited me to play at the Manor."

"More practice is always good," Mami says. She signs the paper with a pen from the pocket of her bright pink work shirt. Over the pocket, black stitching reads *Dream Clean*—the business she started with Señora Reyes when I was younger. "But you're a natural."

"Remember Carmen's wedding?" I ask.

"We'd flown all day. You were tired."

"And Maria's quinceañera?"

She swats the air. "You had the flu—you were dehydrated."

Typical Mami—ignoring the bad. I usually love this about her, like when she never complains about all the extra hours she works to help pay for my private lessons with Mr. Newsum. But what good is pretending that I didn't have two *complete* meltdowns onstage? How is that going to help me *not* have one at my audition?

"What will you play?" Papi asks me.

"Mr. Newsum thinks I should play the Bach pieces I've been working on."

"Ah." Papi leans back in his chair and smiles. "You play him so beautifully."

"Everything she plays is beautiful," Mami says. She starts the dishes and whispers a prayer to the framed picture of Our Lady of Guadalupe hanging above the sink. "La Morenita will be with you. She will give you strength."

Papi and I clear the rest of the plates, and he pulls me in for a hug. His beard tickles my neck and I squirm, but he won't let me go. His arms are strong, his flannel shirt soft—I feel like nothing can go wrong when he has me wrapped up like this.

"Ves estas manos?" he says. He shows me his brown hands. They're strong, with large veins running around knuckles and old scars. "These hands are good at building houses and driving trucks. Now these . . ." He examines mine like a doctor, and kisses the palm of each one. "They were made to play Bach. Now go practice."

In my room, I take the cello out of the case. The wood is very dark, and very old. That's good—cellos get better with time, Mr. Newsum says. He found this one in the back of a repair shop in New York City last year. He was there to get a crack fixed in his double bass, and talked the man down to a good price. My parents surprised me with it last Christmas—the best present I will ever get. I played so many hours that break, my wrists hurt for a month.

I stare at the two dents on the upper bout—one from my cousin Maria's birthday party, one from my cousin Carmen's wedding. I wish Mami was right about them.

But I know better.

I put rosin on my bow to grip the strings, tune, and do one of the breathing exercises that Mr. Newsum sent me— in through the nose for two counts, out of the mouth for a four count. I pretend the Maple Hill string teachers are sitting in my room and run through my scales. Next, I play Popper's Etude #1—a short piece that works on hand positioning and tone. Most string players hate them, but I think they're fun. When I'm all warmed up, I get out the first Bach piece I learned: *Arioso*. It isn't hard, and I know it by heart— perfect to start my set at the Manor on Friday.

I say, "Okay Virgencita de Guadalupe. Help me play this piece as good as it sounds in my head."

Above my desk, the Carlos Prieto poster hangs. His eyes are closed, and his bow is up in the air—I always wonder if he's at the beginning or the end of the piece. Do angry bees swarm his stomach when he goes onstage? Has he ever had a . . . *situation* in front of hundreds of people?

I say, "You're not a saint—but if you're giving out blessings, I'll take all the help I can get."

I set my fingers and count in.

One and

Two and

Ready and

Go.

The piece is slow and a little sad, like flower petals floating to the ground. A gentle breeze lifts them up every now and then, and my fingers take the melody higher. I climb up and down the cello neck, my wrist loose as I create each vibrato—the wobble that gives a note more meaning. I close my eyes, and play softer as I picture the petals landing on the wet grass. My bow slows on the last phrase, and the sound hangs in the air. In a few seconds, it's gone.

I open my eyes. The two dents stare up at me.

Maybe there won't be a third.

I can get over this—I *have* to get over this.

January fourth is only a month away.

8

THAT'S IN LIKE FOUR WEEKS

RONNY

JO is being so weird today. On the bus I tell her about the stupid thing I said to Ms. Q but she's way off in her brain somewhere and just says *yeah* and *oh wow*. She eats lunch in the orchestra room so she can practice for this cello thing at the old people's home on Friday and then after school is going right to string practice without meeting back at our lockers. Okay so you want to go to Maple Hill but come on you're still at this school so what gives?

But whatever because I got FINAL NOTICE problems to figure out like where my mom keeps her bill folder. I checked a bunch of normal places yesterday like the closet and the filing cabinet so it's probably in her room somewhere.

"Hey bud," my dad says when I'm coming home from school. He's at the kitchen on our big family laptop eating Cheez-Its. "How was school?"

"Good," I say and now I'm sitting with him and eating too. He hasn't shaved his head in a while so some of the old hair is growing in where he still has hair. It's weird how up top it's brown like mine but his beard is sort of reddish. "What are you doing?"

"Emailing my old boss, John. Seeing if he has any openings for the spring."

"How's your back?"

He does some shoulder rolling. "Pretty good today."

"That's good," I say and I hope John has zero openings at his stupid lumber place. Why would my dad even want to go back there? He's pretty tall and he's got big arms that could do anything before a forklift fell on him at work.

"Gotta do homework," I say and go to my room.

But I'm really sneaking into him and my mom's room real quiet. I'm over at my mom's side of the bed now and turning on the lamp. She's got this little table thing she brought from our old house with a couple drawers and I check there first.

The top one is just books and stuff so I look in the bigger two on the bottom. More books and no folder which is great just great. Then I see this picture frame turned over and flip it back up. It's of my dad carrying my mom in both arms like he's rescuing her from a burning building or something. It's old because her hair is real long and he still has hair and a big mustache. They're both smiling and laughing and then I see it's right in front of our old house. Like they're by the steps that go up to the front door and he's carrying her up and there's a balloon on the knob and it says *Welcome Home*.

I hear my dad coming down the hall and now I'm duck-ing behind the bed. He's digging around for his workout bands in the closet and now he's in the living room doing his exercises with the news on. I'm taking big breaths because oh man close call but now I'm opening my eyes real wide. There's the blue folder under my mom's little table.

I grab it and go to my room and now I'm looking through bills on the desk until I find FINAL NOTICE.

"Gotcha," I say and right then Bianca stomps in the front door. In like five seconds she's in our room being annoying.

"What are you doing here?" she says.

"I live here."

She's looking over my shoulder at all the papers. "What is that?"

"Homework. Get outta here."

"You never do homework."

"Yeah I'm starting now so gimme some space."

Bianca is folding her arms. "That's my desk."

"It's the only desk."

"But it's from my room."

"Yeah because mine was too big to bring."

She's throwing her stuff on the bottom bunk and going to the bathroom. "Can't you work in the kitchen?" she says.

"You work in the kitchen."

"I have to study for a spelling test."

"They still do that?" I say.

She's flushing now and coming back over. "Why don't you go to Jo's?"

"She's practicing."

"She's always practicing, and you still go."

"Listen Bianca," I say and quick put the folder in my book bag. "You're being kind of annoying so I'm gonna leave and please don't follow me."

"You're being weird."

I go to the bathroom and lock the door but what is that smell?

"Ugh," I say because Bianca didn't flush the toilet again. I press the handle but it just fills up higher and oh man it's near the top. "Gross."

"It won't flush all the way," Bianca yells from our room. "Something's wrong with the toilet."

"How do you even do that?" I say.

"I'll fix it when I'm done with my workout, buddy," my dad says.

"Going to Jo's!" I yell.

I get my coat and walk like twenty feet to Jo's apartment in the freezing cold. I'm slipping on the icy sidewalk because a bunch of rain from last week made everything wet but then it got really cold right after. At our old house there was always salt and stuff on the sidewalks in the winter but not here so what's up with that?

Now I'm knocking on Jo's door and her mom is opening it.

"Ronaldo," she says. "How are you?"

"Pretty good," I say and go in. Jo's playing cello in her room and it sounds amazing as always. "Whoa smells way better here than my house."

"I think he's hungry," Jo's dad says. He fist-bumps me and puts a clean plate on the table.

"Ha no but thanks."

They laugh and Jo's mom gets stuff out of the fridge. "Always with the jokes," she says.

"No really I gotta talk to Jo about this school thing."

"Which class?" her dad says.

"Uh," I say. "Social studies."

"You're too skinny," Mrs. Ramos says. "Are you getting taller?"

"Ha I hope," I say and she's putting a bunch of tortillas on my plate and steaming hot meat that smells amazing. I wrap it up and I'm eating it so fast I burn my mouth. "You should teach all the moms how to make this."

"Carne guisada," Mr. Ramos says. "Say it."

"Carne guisada."

"Excelente. It means 'boiled donkey.'"

"Ha what?" I say and he's laughing so hard at me.

Mrs. Ramos whacks him with a towel and says something else in Spanish. "Marinated steak," she says. "Secret family recipe."

"I mean it's so good I don't care if it was donkey."

I eat another one and now I'm going to Jo's room. She's in the cello zone with her eyes all closed and her arm moving back and forth making this incredible sound. Carlos Prieto is watching her from his poster and on the other wall is Yo-Yo Ma and probably both of them would be really amazed by how good she is.

"Wow really good," I say when she's done.

"Thanks."

I'm just standing there with my book bag and why is this so weird? I come over all the time. "I got big problems I haven't told you about."

She's putting her cello down. "Ronny—I really am sorry. I should've told you that I was even thinking about applying to Maple Hill."

"What?" I say and I'm shaking my head. "This is my mom's giant folder of bills." I'm taking the FINAL NOTICE bill out and showing Jo. "She looks at this stuff every morning before work and sometimes when she comes home. Yesterday I saw her looking at this one really worried."

Jo looks at it. "What's it for?"

"I don't know but FINAL NOTICE is bad when it comes to money stuff. There's like legal action they can do and yeah I'm pretty sure that's why they took our old house away. So what I'm saying is will you help me figure this out?"

"Yes," she says, and it sounds like the old Jo which is good. She smooths out the paper on her desk and we both stare at it. Now she's pointing to a title thing at the top that says *Citadel Credit Union*. "That's the place up by the car wash."

"Oh yeah," I say. "I mean what is it?"

"I think it's like a bank."

"But it says credit union."

"I think they're the same thing," she says.

"Right."

In the middle part there's a lot of spreadsheet boxes with tiny numbers and dates and stuff that makes zero sense but way at the bottom there's a bolded part that's easy to get.

Your LOAN (ACCOUNT #2984325) in the amount of ($878.36) is 150 DAYS past due as of (December 1).

"Whoa," I say and I read the numbers again. "That's a lot of money and a lot of days past due."

Jo is nodding. "But it doesn't say what it's for."

I turn the paper over but it's only a phone number and a website.

"Let's call," I say.

She gets her cell phone out because I don't have one. "What are you going to say?" Jo says.

"I'm gonna ask them what happens if we don't pay it."

It's ringing and now a robot voice is telling me stuff. Jo puts it on speaker and we listen to a bunch of directions and hit zero to talk to a human. We wait a couple seconds and then somebody picks up.

"Citadel Credit Union, this is Bart speaking," says a guy. "Can I have your first and last name."

"Make your voice low," Jo says real quiet. "Like your dad's."

"Listen, Bart," I say real deep like my dad. "This is Mark Russo with a money problem."

"Can I have your loan number?"

"Loan number," I say and Jo is pointing to the number in the middle of the page. "Yeah here it is."

I read it to him.

"Thank you," he says and there's a lot of typing. "And can I have your address?" I give him that too and he types some more. "And the last four digits of your social security number."

I look at Jo real confused and she's hitting the mute button. "That's the special number you get."

"From who?"

"The government," she says. "My parents and I each have a card in a fire box under my dad's bed."

"Pretty sure I'd know if I had a special government number," I say but wait would I? I didn't know a lot of stuff like you could just lose your house to a giant orange sticker but that happened.

"Mr. Russo?" Bart says.

I hit the button to unmute. "Listen Bart I lost it okay?"

"Oh, I'm sorry to hear that sir."

"Yeah it's these dang kids," I say and Jo is thinking real hard. "Always taking stuff out of my wallet."

"Yes sir, I understand. But unfortunately, I need that number to verify your identity."

"But it's me, Mark Russo."

"Yes, sir, but it's the law," Bart says. "I can only give account information to a verified account holder."

Now Jo is pointing at the FINAL NOTICE part.

"Okay but Bart," I say. "What's does it mean if my bill says FINAL NOTICE?"

He's not talking for a second and now he's using that adult voice like he knows I'm not my dad. "Well *sir*, that would mean your account is in delinquency."

"Whoa that's a big word."

"*It means in trouble*," Jo says real quiet.

"It means we haven't received a payment for your loan in five months," Bart says.

"Right and that's bad," I say. "So what happens now?"

"Our automobile loans have a six-month delinquency period."

I'm looking at Jo and my eyes are going crazy wide.

Automobile loans.

Cars.

"Six months," I say.

"That is when the car will be repossessed which means—"

Now Jo's eyes are real wide and my brain is spinning on *repossessed* because I heard that back when the bank put that orange sticker on our house. "Like you're gonna take it."

"If the payment has not been made, sir."

It's quiet for a while and I'm hearing Jo's parents watching Spanish TV in the living room. "Come on, Bart, you can't do that," I say but I forget to use my fake dad voice.

"I'm sorry . . . kid. Those are the terms of our auto loans."

"But we already sold our other car."

"Listen—"

"My mom needs it for her job," I say real loud. "She works late a lot and the bus doesn't run then."

"I understand, son," Bart says.

Jo grabs the phone and hangs up. I'm squinting hard and trying to do calendar math but my brain is spinning like crazy on *repossession*.

On January 1.

That's in like four weeks.

9

STAGE FRIGHT

JO

"HOMEMADE brownies," Esther announces. Seventh graders walk by our bake sale table on the way into the cafeteria. "Dark chocolate, regular, and blondie. One dollar each."

Three girls stop by, inspecting our selection. They each buy one, and I mark their hands with a cello stamp. "Thanks for supporting the string ensemble," I say.

"I thought this was for the musical," one of the girls says.

"That was last month."

"And they sold cookies," Esther says.

"Do you guys have any cookies?" another girl asks.

Esther looks at me with one eyebrow raised. "No," she tells them. "Just a variety of delicious brownies."

They leave, and Esther takes a bite of her tuna sandwich. I'm hungry too, but my stomach is an active beehive—tomorrow I perform at the Manor. This morning I put my permission slip on Mrs. Vargas's piano in the choir room so I couldn't change my mind. There is no backing out now.

Ronny walks out of the cafeteria with a kid bigger than most teachers: Mason. Everything about him is large—arms, legs, stomach. He wears his usual sweatpants and brown leather jacket that his grandfather gave him.

"Come on, food is a waste of money," Ronny tells him. He shows Mason something in his unzipped book bag. "Xbox controllers are way better."

Mason studies the brownies. He scratches a mountain of blond curly hair. "How much?"

"One dollar," Esther says.

Ronny shakes his head. "You can get a brownie anywhere."

"Actually, you can't," Esther says. "They're not as common as you'd think."

Mason buys two and gives one to Ronny. They sit on the hallway floor next to our table and eat them.

"Thanks," Ronny says, but he sounds upset. He left my house quickly last night—right after we called that man from the bank. On the bus this morning, he drew circles on the window and wouldn't talk to me. "But you could've bought my controllers for the rock-bottom price of five dollars. Probably I would have taken two dollars."

I say, "Isn't your Xbox broken?"

"The box part yeah but the controllers still work."

"Two bucks isn't fair," Mason says. "That would be like stealing them."

"Yeah but I'm selling them to you so it's fine."

"What do you need the money for?" Esther asks.

Ronny looks right at me—just for a second. But in that one second, I understand him perfectly.

Don't. Say. Anything.

"Gonna get my Xbox fixed," he tells Esther.

"But you're selling the controllers," she says.

"Yeah because I can't use them if there's no Xbox, duh."

"You should get a job for the holidays," Mason says. "People do that."

I say, "You need to be thirteen, I think."

"Great, just great," Ronny says.

I count the money we've made so far today—eighteen dollars. As I do, I realize just how much eight hundred and seventy-eight dollars is.

Is Ronny *really* trying to raise that much by selling his own stuff?

Ronny stares at the money box. "You guys aren't thirteen," he says. "How come you can sell brownies?"

"This isn't a job," Esther says. "It's a fundraiser."

"Yeah but come on, it's the same thing."

"We're not getting paid."

"Actually, he's right," Mason says. "The money goes to the string ensemble, which goes eventually to you for bus travel and equipment."

I say, "I never thought of it like that."

Ronny squints even harder—his eyes are almost invisible. "How come your parents don't just give the money to Mr. Newsum to buy that stuff? Like why do all the work to buy the brownie mix and make them?"

"Because a box of brownie mix is cheaper than the fresh

brownies you make with it," Mason explains to him. "They're selling them at a dollar a brownie, so that's at least twelve dollars per box. How much is one at the store, Esther?"

"One dollar and twenty-nine cents," she says.

"Whoa," Ronny says. "So a dollar turns into twelve. That's like really good."

"Hola Josefina." I look toward the voice and see Mrs. Vargas, the choir director. She and another teacher stand by the water bottle filling station. "Got your permission slip, thanks for joining us! The Manor residents will love it!"

"My gram used to live there," Ronny says. "They have these drink machines and you can get as much as you want, it was awesome."

Mrs. Vargas and the other teacher walk away.

"Are you gonna barf?" Ronny asks me. "Your face looks weird."

The back of my throat tastes like sour chocolate. I do a breathing count—two in, four out. Lying is way less embarrassing. But I'm so scared about tomorrow that saying it out loud seems like the best idea in the whole world.

I say, "I have very, very bad stage fright."

"Like you pee your pants?" Ronny asks.

"You're thinking of weak bladder syndrome," Mason tells him. "Which is pretty common. If anyone here has that."

"I don't," I say.

"Did you try those breathing exercises from Mr. Newsum?" Esther asks me.

I nod. "But this isn't just nervous butterflies—it's a swarming beehive that gets bigger and bigger until I can't play. Can breathing exercises fix that?"

"I don't get it," Ronny says. "You play in front of people all the time and you're never freaking out."

I say, "It's only when I do a solo."

Two boys come out to our table, and Esther sells them each a brownie. My stomach grumbles—I finally feel like eating. I take a bite, and chew slowly. This could be the best brownie in the world.

"So how bad is it?" Esther asks me.

"Two summers ago, I dropped my cello at my cousin's wedding," I say. "I was so nervous, the neck slipped out of my hand as she was walking down the aisle. Everyone in the church looked away from her and stared at me."

"Oh man," Ronny says.

"I went to get it, but my dress caught on the chair—I almost fell out. And when I finally picked it up, the whole thing was out of tune. My cousin had to walk down the rest of the way in complete silence."

Esther slides me another brownie. "Get it all out."

I eat the whole thing in two bites—Ronny style. "Last summer, I almost blinded my uncle at a birthday party."

Mason coughs on the water he's sipping.

"I was playing too fast—I was so nervous," I say. "I lost track of the measures and started missing notes. My string crossings squeaked, and I was trying to get back on track when my fingers just . . . lost control. The bow went flying and hit my uncle in the eye."

"Come on no," Ronny says. "Probably this is a joke."

"Not a joke."

His eyes get very big—he gets it now. "Oh man you gotta do solos to get into the cello school for champions."

"That's why she's playing at the Manor," Esther tells him.

"Trial by fire," Mason says. "That's a pretty good strategy."

"Okay okay okay," Ronny says. "You'll get some good practice with the old people and you'll be okay for the audition."

I say, "Or I have another *situation*."

Ronny plays with his empty brownie ziplock bag—hitting it into the air like a balloon.

Then he lets it drop.

"Wait, I'll sit up there like your assistant or something. I mean your music has a ton of pages so I can turn them but really I'm there to catch your cello if you drop it and stop people from getting stabbed in the eye by your bow."

"A cello wingman," Mason says. "I support this."

I say, "Okay. Thanks."

"And I can sell brownies," Ronny says. "Old people love brownies."

"Everyone loves brownies," Esther says. "But you can't charge old people for food at a charity concert."

"You're actually not supposed to say 'old people,'" Mason says. "You're supposed to say 'senior citizens.'"

"Guys, come on," Ronny says. "If you can sell brownies to

kids for cello stuff, then I can sell them to old people for my Xbox fixing."

In the cafeteria, Mr. Killroy announces that it's time to clean up. I say, "You should check with Mrs. Vargas to see if it's okay for you to come."

"How much is it to fix your Xbox?" Mason asks.

Ronny looks at me again—another long second. "A lot."

10

TAHITIAN BLUE IS STUPID

RONNY

"I miss going to see Gram at that old people's place," I say. "Like before she died. I mean it smelled weird but everybody was always happy to see us."

"Me too, buddy." My dad is stirring pasta on the stove and reading over the permission slip. I got it from Mrs. Vargas after lunch but I definitely did not ask about the brownies because no way she was gonna say yes. "So what time is this thing over? Is the bus taking you back to school?"

"Yeah and Jo's mom is bringing me home."

"What's this for again?"

"She's doing a cello thing after the choir sings and I'm her page turner," I say but I need to say something about brownies because I'm gonna be making them tonight. "Yeah and I'm supposed to bring brownies to hand out to them."

"That's fun—Bianca, dinner in five," he says and he's pouring the hot water out over the drainer thing in the sink but some is splashing up and burning his hands. He jumps back real quick and, oh man, he's falling but now he's grabbing the counter to not wipe out.

"Whoa are you okay?"

"All good," he says and he's rubbing his back pretty hard. "I don't know if we have any brownie mix, bud."

"Yeah I know," I say because I checked right away when I got home today. "I was gonna go get a box at the Foodmart place by the gas station and make them after dinner."

My dad is going real slow to the top freezer and gets a special belt thing that wraps around the bottom part of his back. "Mom is pretty strict on the grocery budget."

"Yeah but I got a bunch of quarters and brownies are only like one dollar for a box."

Bianca comes in reading a big giant book with a spider on the front. "Where's Mom?"

"Double shift at the hospital," my dad says. "She'll be home pretty late."

"She makes her special mac and cheese on Thursdays."

"I'm on it, Bee."

"With the bacon bits and extra cheese."

He's pulling the bacon bits and cheese out and waving them at her. Now he's dishing us all a bowl and putting them on the table at our spots. Bianca dumps in the extra stuff and takes a big bite.

"Well?" he says.

"Good."

He lifts his spoon up and they clang them together over the table. You can tell he's hurting bad because he's sitting weird in his chair like to one side and leaning on the table.

"Did you know: There's an insect in Virginia called the

wheel bug," Bianca says. "It has a long nose like a needle, and it sticks it into other bugs and sucks their guts out."

"Your brain isn't right," I say.

"Like this." Bianca sticks a straw in her milk cup and sucks it all up. "Like that."

"You need to see like ten doctors."

"That is pretty gross," my dad says.

"This is why she's always waking me up with weird bug dreams."

"Be right back, guys," he says and is getting up real slow. "Gonna stretch out for a little. Keep eating." He goes to his room but instead of stretching I hear the big squeaking of him laying down in his bed.

"Probably there's a place for you," I say. "Like where the families are freaked out by their kids so they make them leave."

Bianca is sticking her tongue out. "At least I don't have nightmares like you."

"Yeah about cheese. Probably I have powers because they had none at school after I had my dream about it."

She's shaking her head. "People are trying to hurt you in your nightmares. You yell 'No!'"

"What? No I don't."

"Something bad is happening in your dreams."

"You're crazy," I say because pretty sure I'd know if I was having nightmares. But Bianca never remembers talking about animals so maybe I wouldn't remember either? "Do I do it a lot?"

She's thinking about it. "Like once a month."

That seems like a lot. "Wake me up next time so I can remember what I'm dreaming about and it'll stop happening."

"I don't think you can control your nightmares."

"Just do it, okay."

Bianca goes back to the TV room with her bug encyclopedia and I'm putting the stretchy plastic stuff over my dad's food. I make my mom a huge bowl too because she's always starving when she gets home from a double shift. Now I'm back in my room getting my gpop's wallet from the desk. It's black leather and really old and stretched out from all the cool stuff he used to keep in there like mints and golf tees. I'm dumping it out on the desk and count almost ten bucks in some one-dollar bills and quarters which is plenty for brownies.

"Going to the store with Jo," I say through my dad's door and I can hear him groaning and stretching. "To get the brownie stuff."

"Okay bud. Come straight back."

Bianca follows me to the front door. "Liar."

"Bug off and that is a pun."

"Jo goes to her aunt's house in the city on Thursdays."

"Yeah well you probably weren't gonna come with me and then dad would say I couldn't go."

"Can we get ice cream?" Bianca says.

"No."

She's folding her arms. "I want ice cream."

"Okay fine but it can't be more than a dollar."

I tell my dad she's coming with me and we're getting our coats on. It's freezing outside and we go around the back of our building to the street. All the people on the second floor have stairs and they keep stuff on it like a garage. Way down I see the other buildings just like ours and then a bunch more. Probably there's twenty really long two-story houses in this whole place so why do they even call them apartments?

We go across the street to the sidewalk and walk along the big giant white fence that separates the Apartments from the back of the townhomes. They're like skyscrapers way high up looking down on everything and we keep walking right past the one we used to live in. I'm looking up at my old room window but the light's off so maybe the kid who lives there now is in the kitchen or the cool basement where we had our TV. Probably his mom has brownie mix built into the strict food budget and so he doesn't have to go out with his little sister in the freezing cold dark to get it.

"We used to have real bacon with mac and cheese," Bianca says. "And mom used to make it with different noodles. And she'd bake it in the oven."

"Yeah, it was way better."

She's looking back at our old house. "I wonder if the new family found the secret cubby in the hallway where Mom and Dad put the Christmas presents."

"Yeah," I say. It's probably stuffed with cool stuff that we won't be getting this year. "That was a good spot."

"I remember the upstairs bathroom always clogged there too."

"Probably that was just something that happened with you."

We keep going and now we're squinting in the crazy bright lights of the Foodmart and gas station. I never came here when we lived in the townhomes but kids from the Apartments go back and forth all the time which is now me, ha. It has all the regular stuff like coffee and slushies and all the energy drinks but lots of other stuff like paper towels and toilet paper.

We're inside and Bianca is going right for the corner where they have the ice cream. I'm going up and down the little rows and bingo I find the brownie mix right away. There's only one kind and it's $3.50 so what gives? Now I'm reading the directions and it says I need an egg.

"Bianca, do we have any eggs?" I say real loud.

"I don't know."

Great just great. Probably eggs are gonna be expensive too. I can't ask Jo for one because she's not home.

"We're out of eggs," the skinny worker guy says. He's waving at me from the counter where you pay.

I'm going up to him. He's got long hair and sort of a beard that's covering up a bunch of red patches on his face. "Like you have zero eggs here?"

"Yeah. We had a lot but somebody dropped them."

"I really need some eggs."

"It was me," he says. "I dropped them. Slipped on the floor after I mopped it."

Bianca comes over with this giant ice cream bar thing. "This is only two dollars."

"Which is more than one dollar," I say.

She goes away to get something else.

"So it's for a bake sale," I say. "I'm making brownies and I need an egg."

The guy is scratching his face and looking around the store. His name tag says *Glenn* and probably he's in college or maybe a little older. "We're having a sale on candy."

"But I need an egg."

"People like candy too," Glenn says. "Maybe more than brownies."

"What?" I say but then I'm getting it. "Like sell the candy instead of the brownies."

"Yeah." He's pointing to the big candy rack behind me. "All king-size chocolate bars are on sale for fifty cents. That's two for a dollar."

I'm doing the numbers in my head and yeah this will work. Maybe I would've burnt the brownies so this is way better actually. "Old people eat candy bars, right?"

"Everybody eats candy bars."

Bianca comes up and is frowning big-time at me. "There's no ice cream for one dollar."

"You can have one of these," I say and I'm grabbing all different kinds of candy bars and putting them on the counter.

I keep going until I get to sixteen and now I'm paying Glenn with all my quarters and dollar bills.

We start walking back and Bianca is eating her king-size Hershey's bar. I got fifteen left so if I sell them for $1 I'll make $15. Maybe I should sell them for $2 and make $30 because that's way closer to $878.

Bianca stops at the back of our old townhouse again and is she waving? I look up and there's this girl in Bianca's old room waving back at us so I wave too. Then she goes away but Bianca is still staring at her old window like I do sometimes.

"Charlotte Finley," Bianca says.

"You know her?"

"She's in two of my classes."

"You switch classes in fifth grade?"

"Only for reading and math."

"Oh right." I'm looking way up at my old window now because the light went on. "Does she have a brother or sister or something?"

"An older brother. He goes to a private school."

"Oh," I say and that's actually pretty good because man it would be weird if both of them were in our classes.

Bianca is looking at me and she's got chocolate on her face. "She painted my room this color called Tahitian blue. Right over the big unicorn Dad stenciled for me. She talked about it during morning meeting one time. She said it's like waking up every day looking at the Caribbean Ocean."

She's blinking now and two big tears come out. She wipes

them and it mixes with the chocolate and it smears all over her cheeks.

I'm hugging her now and squeezing real hard. "Tahitian blue is stupid."

"Yeah."

"And like what even is the Caribbean Ocean?"

"It's a body of water near Jamaica."

"Yeah but unicorns are way better."

She's wiping her face and nodding. "Unicorns are awesome."

"Yeah everybody knows unicorns are awesome and Tahitian blue is stupid."

We cross the street and go back on the snow path to our apartment. Later when I'm going to bed I look out the window and see TV lights coming from my old room. Probably it's one of those giant ones with the real good picture and the kid has a ton of his private school friends over all the time to watch movies on it.

I'm doing lots of not sleeping but then I'm dreaming about a tow truck dragging our car and the driver is a unicorn? Then Bianca is shaking me and saying stuff real quiet.

"Ronny. You were yelling."

I'm just staring at her in the dark for a while because oh man that dream was so real. "I was?"

"Yeah. What was it?"

"What?"

"Your dream," she says. "You said wake you up so you remember what it was about."

"I don't know," I say which is sort of true because a unicorn driving?

Bianca goes back to her bed and is snoring in like zero time. I get some water in the kitchen and now I'm looking out the front window to make sure our car is still there.

11

SWEAT

JO

I stand outside the front doors of the Manor. Cold wind blows, but I feel hot. My long-sleeve black concert dress sticks to my skin under the winter coat.

"You're gonna do awesome," Ronny tells me. "Probably people will be talking about how awesome you did for a lot of years."

Be ye not afraid of the unknown, Mr. Newsum said.

I inhale for two counts, and then exhale for four.

"Okay," I say. "Let's go."

I step forward and the automatic doors slide open.

Inside, we follow the choir to a large welcome room with string lights and decorations. Mrs. Vargas talks with a white woman wearing a white polo shirt and black jeans. She has gray hair pulled back in a ponytail but doesn't look much older than Mami. The name tag on her shirt says *SARAH: Community Director.*

I say, "Is it hot in here?" I take off my coat.

"Yeah, old people like everything hot," Ronny tells me.

"My gram was always asking who left a door open and could somebody turn up the dang heat. And like they want their coffee and food basically on fire."

Ms. Sarah checks something on her clipboard, and then leads everyone down the hallway to a sitting room she calls the Lounge. Rows of chairs fill the space in front of a big TV hanging on the wall. Nearby, I hear the clang of silverware and see cafeteria workers wiping down tables across the hall. I put my cello down and sit with Ronny in the back row. Nurses in green uniforms like the ones Ronny's mom wears help residents to their seats. Mrs. Vargas and the choir wait in the back.

"Do you want some juice?" Ronny says.

I feel dizzy. "No."

"Okay, I'm gonna go talk to some people."

The seats are filled—forty people, at least. Mrs. Vargas plays a note on the pitch finder, and the choir hums. I take deep, two-count inhales through my nose and exhale for four.

I can do this.

Down the row, I see Ronny talking to a resident with very dark brown skin and curly hair the color of snow. Ronny laughs at something she said, and then shows her his open backpack. She reaches her hand in and comes out with . . . a candy bar. It's thick and has a silver wrapping with red lettering.

A few nearby residents peek in the bag too. Ronny explains

something to them, and they each take a candy bar. He looks over and smiles at me so wide that I can't help but smile back—until I see the nurse come up behind him.

"What are you doing?" she asks loudly. She snatches the candy bars out of the residents' hands. The first woman with the snowy hair won't give it back—the nurse has to pry it out of her hands.

"Testing, testing," says Ms. Sarah over the microphone. The back lights dim, and people stop talking. "Welcome, residents, to Friday Social Hour. We are *very* excited to have with us tonight the Kennesaw Middle School a capella group led by Mrs. Vargas. Some holiday favorites are in store. Let's give them a warm welcome."

The residents clap. The beehive rumbles.

Ms. Sarah consults her clipboard. "And after the caroling, we have a *special* cello performance by a member of the Kennesaw string ensemble, Josefina Ramos."

They clap again. I shrink lower in my seat.

"Oh—one more thing," Ms. Sarah says. "There will be cookies and tapioca pudding in the cafeteria afterwards for audience and performers alike. Sugar free, of course."

The residents groan.

Ronny plops down next to me. He frowns.

"What were you doing?" I whisper. "What happened?"

"Nurse Monica ruined everything is what happened." He looks over at the nurse who took the candy bars. I watch her whisper to Ms. Sarah and point in our direction. She has his backpack. "But maybe she also saved me from going to jail."

"What?"

The choir starts their first song. Harmonies fill the room and distract the beehive inside me. They are good—I even sing along. But as each one ends, the hive vibrates more. After they finish their fifth song, I take my cello down the hallway to tune. Ronny follows me out.

"How do I know when to turn the music page?" Ronny asks.

"I'll nod."

"Okay. Wait, like a big nod or a little nod?"

"Just a normal nod."

"Right, okay."

I say, "What were you doing with that candy?"

"Oh man." He tears open a king-size Kit Kat bar and bites into it. "I'll tell you later."

The choir finishes their last song. I roll up the sleeves of my dress to try and cool down—I'm a furnace. "Ronny, I can't do this," I say.

"Yeah, you can." He breaks me off a piece of the Kit Kat bar. "This will give you energy."

Applause echoes down the hall. It's almost time.

"If I eat that, I will throw it up onstage."

He puts the rest in his pocket. "You're the greatest cello player ever, okay."

"No—I'm not."

"Come on who's better than you?"

"Thousands of people," I say. "And they don't have this kind of stage fright."

He nods. "Okay if you mess up—but you won't because you're amazing—I'll beat up anybody who laughs at you even if it's an old person. I took karate so I can do that stuff."

"You think they'll *laugh* at me?" I say. "Why would you say that?"

"No, I mean like if they do—"

"*Josefina*," Mrs. Vargas whispers down the hall. "*You're on.*"

My cello feels like a hundred pounds as I walk to the front of the Lounge. I sit in the chair slowly, afraid that I might drop it—again. Ronny puts my music on the stand and sits next to me. I shuffle the sheets until I find *Arioso*. Sweat drips off my forehead and lands on the cello.

I look at the residents and try to smile. The woman with the snowy hair winks at me. I set my fingers on the strings and raise my bow arm.

I count myself in.

One and

Two and

Ready and

Go.

Dahhhhhhhhh, da da da, daaaaaaa, dadada daaaa da da daaaaaaa da da da daaa dada dahhhhhh.

Da—

Sweat splashes on the A string right where my pinkie lands. The note wobbles, and then slips totally out of key.

My down bow stops in the middle of the string crossing, which makes a horrible *screeeeeeeech*.

I freeze.

"Do I turn the page now?" Ronny whispers.

I shake my head.

He turns it anyway.

I wipe my left hand on my dress and restart the phrase.

Daaaaaaa—

But I'm sharp. How am I *sharp*? I've played that note a thousand times and it's *never* been sharp. Am I playing the right note? Did I shift out of key? Is it the heat in this room?

I look at the music—wrong page. Sweat drips into my eye, and I wipe my face. The choir stares at me, mouths wide-open. A nurse in the back drinks from a cup. I've never wanted juice so badly in my entire life.

A very old white woman in the front row coughs. Tubes run into her nose and down to an oxygen tank next to her. It makes a quiet *cushhh* sound every few seconds.

Cushhh.

Cushhh.

Cushhh.

She glares at me, angry that I've ruined the concert.

Cushhh.

Cushhh.

Cushhh.

12

JO IS ACTUALLY REALLY GOOD

RONNY

"JO," I say real low but she is way gone. She is pretty much a statue of a sweating person playing the cello. Man her eyes are real wide and her mouth is kind of open like she saw a dead person or maybe that lady in the front row making a scary face.

"So," I say real loud. "So I mean—" And now I'm standing up in front of Jo. "Right like so how about that choir? Let's clap again for them. I mean they were great."

Everybody just keeps staring at Jo.

"Ha okay," I say and I'm trying to get that Sarah lady's attention to get Jo the heck out of here. I mean somebody help us out here like these people are adults, right?

"I mean singing without music ha that's weird," I say. "Right? Haha. It's like come on, Mrs. Vargas. Some drums or something would be nice."

Mrs. Vargas is giving me big frowns.

Now the Sarah lady is coming up and takes Jo's cello. They walk off real slow and go over to a table at the cafeteria place across the hall. People were watching them for a little but now they're all looking at me.

"So yeah singing with no instruments is pretty weird," I say. "Like we can all agree on that right."

"I got a question," says Rebecca. She's the really nice old Black lady who I tried to sell candy to. "Where's my Chunky Monkey?"

"Ha yeah good question," I say. "Funny story okay. So I brought some candy with me. Big candy bars like the king-size ones I got on sale. I was gonna sell them to you guys."

Nurse Monica is shaking her head at me in the way back.

"They're really good ones," I say. "Real big ones. Kit Kat. Hershey's. Chunky Monkey. All the regular ones. I bought them for fifty cents at the Foodmart and I was selling them for two dollars here. It was for . . . a fundraiser for the orchestra to buy strings and stuff."

Some of them are nodding like they feel bad.

"Okay no," I say. "I'm too young to get a job so I was trying to make some money to get my Xbox fixed. Like it was a fundraiser for my bank account."

A couple of the old people laugh.

"Yeah but turns out you can't sell candy to old people—I mean, senior citizens," I say.

Now a bunch more are laughing.

"Not that you guys don't like candy," I say. "Like you were all over it, but Monica told me I couldn't give it to you."

An old guy dressed up real nice with a tie on is raising

his hand. "I'll trade you a tapioca pudding for some of that Hershey's bar."

"Ha sold," I say, and everybody is laughing now. It feels good because maybe they forgot about Jo totally freaking out. "No but really I can't give you candy because of this thing called diabetes that my gram used to have."

"I got it too," says the same old guy and a bunch of them are nodding. "A lot of us do."

"Yeah it's pretty serious and Nurse Monica says a giant chocolate bar would probably kill you."

Like every actual person in the room is laughing now. Even Nurse Monica is covering her mouth and squinting. I'm looking at Sarah in the cafe who is getting Jo a cup of juice and she's laughing.

But Jo isn't.

She's just staring at her juice.

"So I just wanted to help my school—I mean myself," I say, "and if it wasn't for Nurse Monica I'd probably be arrested right now. But probably it would be really good and better than that sugar-free pudding you guys have to eat."

The room is going crazy. The old guy with the nice clothes is bending over and slapping his knee. Only that mean lady in the front isn't getting in on this and probably because she's got all those tubes in her nose.

"How about that choir with no instruments," I say and clap and they all clap and keep laughing. Now Sarah is back up onstage and I walk real quick to check on Jo.

"Yes, how about that choir," Sarah says. "Mrs. Vargas—could we do another round of 'God Bless Ye Merry Gentlemen'?"

"Oh man are you okay?" I say. "Did I mess you up with the page turning?"

"No," Jo says and she's got her head on the table with both arms folded. Now she's looking up and grabbing my wrist real hard. "Thank you. I was dying up there."

"Yeah but you're okay right?"

She's just shaking her head. "I knew this would happen."

"Yeah but it sounded really good what you played."

"Four measures."

"Probably the rest would've been just as amazing."

"Ronny—I choked."

"I'll get some more juice," I say.

I get her cup and fill it back up. All the residents are coming over now and getting served sugar-free pudding so I get one of those for us too. Jo eats some of hers but mostly just stares at the table.

This old lady is coming over real slow with one of those walker things. It's got tennis balls on the bottom so it kind of slides. "That was lovely," she says to Jo. "Just lovely. Thank you."

Jo is trying to smile but it looks weird.

"Yeah wait till she plays a whole song," I say. "It's really amazing. Probably it's the best cello you ever heard."

"Oh, that will be delightful," the old lady says.

Other old people come up and say nice things but Jo is

faking pretty good and just nodding. It's like she's melting or something and every second it's more embarrassing. Now Nurse Monica is coming by pushing that mean lady in a wheelchair with all the tubes and the machine that makes noise.

"Children, in the cafe," she says. "Inappropriate."

"Ha," I say. "Yup."

"Now, Noreen," Nurse Monica says like she's embarrassed by the lady. "These are guests."

Noreen is shaking her head and making mean faces at us. "Inappropriate."

"I'm going to pack up," Jo says and she's walking real fast to get her cello.

"Hey cool pin," I say and point at the sparkly flower on Noreen's sweater. "Is that like a rose?"

Noreen is looking down at the pin and touches it with her hand. "A child, in the cafe."

"Okay, Noreen," says Nurse Monica. "Let's go cheer up someone else."

I eat the rest of my pudding and then Jo's pudding and wash it down with three cups of juice. I go back to the Lounge to find Jo but she's not there and her cello is gone too.

Sarah is stacking chairs and waves me over. "Wanna give me a hand?"

"Yeah," I say and help her do a bunch. "Where's Jo?"

"I think she went outside."

"Okay."

"Hey, that was pretty cool," she says. "Jumping in there when she was having some trouble."

"Yeah she's actually really good. I'm serious she's gonna be the next Carlos Prieto."

"*Really.*"

"Wait you know who that is?"

Sarah is nodding. "I have a cousin who studied the violin. He actually did a workshop with Carlos's son, Miguel. He's a famous orchestra director, you know."

"Ha wow. Yeah Jo's gonna be like them. She's working on solo stuff so she can get into a special school for kids who love music."

I get my coat on and check outside but no Jo. The bus is there but nobody's on it so now I'm going back inside down a hallway where they have these birds in a cage and some chairs. My gram used to sit in there to read sometimes and I think maybe Jo is hiding there but it's empty too.

I'm walking back to the cafe when I hear the song Jo was gonna play tonight. It's real quiet and coming from way down the other hallway. Sarah hears it too and now she's following me toward the sound. We go around a corner and see a couple nurses standing outside a door looking at something. It's Jo in this tiny office with a couple computers and nurse clipboards and she's just playing. She's got her back to the door and she's way into the song and doesn't even know we're here.

I sit on the floor and listen to her crushing it. I feel a

hundred times better because they're getting to see the real Jo Ramos. But also that sweaty statue thing was really bad and how is she gonna stop that from happening again?

Sarah is watching with her mouth open like *wow* and now she's looking down at me like *Ronny, she is so good.*

"I told you she was good," I say real quiet.

13

THE OFFER

JO

"**WAS** it that bad?" Esther whispers to me.

"Yes."

At the front of the stage, Mr. Newsum explains to the violins that they are still sharp at measure fifteen. Their intonation struggles have eaten up most of fifth period.

"Maybe it felt worse than it actually was," Esther says.

"It felt exactly how it was—awful. Terrible. Humiliating. Defeating—"

"Okay, I get it."

All weekend I didn't leave my room—except to eat and go to Sunday Mass. I played *Arioso* thirty times in a row without missing a note. Ronny came over to cheer me up, and also to eat. After I told Mami what he did for me at the Manor, she made him fresh tortillas smothered with butter.

I say, "My dress felt like a sleeping bag. I was so hot."

"That's why I play in shorts." Esther practices the fingering for a tricky run at the end of the piece. She wipes her forehead with the sweatband on her wrist. "And wear one of these. I'll bring you one to wear next time."

Next time? How can there be a *next* time after *last* time?

The bell rings, and Mr. Newsum dismisses us to lunch.

"Jo-Jo Ma," Mr. Newsum calls after me. "Go get Ronny and swing back to my office with your lunches. Let's chat."

"Why?"

He shrugs like he has no idea, and then talks with Dillon, our double bass player.

"Do you think Mrs. Vargas told him about what happened?" I ask Esther.

"Maybe?"

"Great."

We put our cellos away and stop by Esther's locker for her lunch. In the cafeteria, I get my food and join them back at our lunch table.

"Two bucks," Ronny tells Mason. "Come on, that's a good price."

Mason looks into Ronny's backpack. "Why are they all wrinkled?"

"I been carrying them around since Friday."

Esther examines the candy. "That Hershey's bar is open."

"Oh whoops," Ronny says. He takes it out and eats a piece. "So are you gonna buy some or what?"

"Where'd you get them?" Mason asks.

"The Foodmart place by the gas station."

"How about a dollar?"

"Fine."

I say, "Ronny. Mr. Newsum wants to see us."

"Why?"

"He didn't say."

But I know.

"He better be in the mood to buy some candy," Ronny says. He zips his backpack and we sign out at the front table by Mr. Killroy. "I really need to get rid of these before they get more gross."

"How many did you sell?"

"Not enough. Mostly I been eating them."

In the orchestra closet, Mr. Newsum swivels his chair toward us. "Well, well, well." The room smells like tuna fish. A soccer game plays on his school laptop screen. "Look who it is."

"Okay listen." Ronny lays out three king-size Reese's Peanut Butter Cups on Mr. Newsum's desk. "I will give you these for the crazy low price of six dollars."

"Can't. Peanut butter allergy."

"Oh man come on."

"The only thing between me and a fatal allergic reaction is a thin sheet of plastic wrapper." Mr. Newsum searches in his desk for a handful of quarters and gives them to Ronny. "But my fiancée loves them. I will surprise her with these and secure her love *forever*."

I say, "Mrs. Vargas told you what happened."

Mr. Newsum uses two pieces of paper like gloves and carries the candy to his bag. "She did."

"It was . . . not good."

"Come on it wasn't that bad," Ronny says. "I mean it was bad but it wasn't really *really* bad. Probably it was just regular bad."

"Not what I heard," Mr. Newsum says. He smiles wide—the way Papi does when I play Bach. "I heard it was *incredible.*"

I blink. What is he *talking* about?

I say, "No, it wasn't. I didn't even finish the piece."

Mr. Newsum presses a few buttons on his room phone. A recorded message plays over the speaker.

Hi—Mr. Newsum. Sarah Williams here, Community Director at the Manor. I was just reaching out to say how much the residents—actually the whole staff, to be quite honest—enjoyed Friday's performance. Everyone is still talking about it. I know your cellist, Josefina, got a little nervous, but a few of us heard her play afterward and I have to say she is very talented. Just really something.

Anyway—we'd love to have her come back. Her friend Ronny said she was trying to get some solo experience for an upcoming audition? That seems like a win-win to me. Speaking of Ronny: That kid is hysterical.

"Ha," Ronny says. "We should play this for Ms. Q."

Mr. Newsum shushes him with a finger. The message continues:

He mentioned needing a job for the holidays, so I've got an opportunity he might be interested in. It's a little . . . unconventional, but I think it might fit him. Okay, well, have a great day and I'll send over my email to you. Bye-bye.

Mr. Newsum folds his arms. "Jo-Jo Ma. Ronny: Do you accept?"

"Affirmative," Ronny answers.

I say, "She only heard me play four measures."

"No we heard you play the whole thing," he tells me. "When you went and hid in that office a couple nurses found you and me and Sarah listened too."

"I didn't hear anyone."

"Yeah you were in the Carlos Prieto zone where stuff could explode but you wouldn't know."

"Which piece?" Mr. Newsum asks me.

"*Arioso.*"

I think back to that empty office. I *had* to play that piece all the way through—it was the only thing that made me feel better.

But it also felt . . . *important*. It mattered somehow—it felt *bigger* than me and my stage issues.

"Bach never disappoints," Mr. Newsum says. He writes an email address on a sticky note and holds it out to me. "If you take the gig, we can prep during your lesson this week. I dug into my grad school binder and found a few more performance strategies to review."

"I don't know if I can go back there," I say. Just thinking about it makes my face hot.

"Jo," Ronny says.

And then he walks out of the room—he just leaves. Mr. Newsum and I both look at the empty spot where he was.

"I think he wants to talk with just *you*," Mr. Newsum whispers.

I walk out into the hall. Ronny stands a few feet away.

"Come here," he says.

I step closer.

"You gotta do this."

I play with my braid. "Ms. Sarah might still hire you if I don't come back. I know why you want the job—you're trying to pay the car bill."

"Yeah but you gotta pay soon too," Ronny says. "Not like money, but with stage skills. You only have a couple weeks to get them or those Maple Hill people are gonna take away your cello dreams."

I stare at him, confused.

But then I see myself onstage, playing for the string faculty. They make notes on their clipboards when I mess up, and shake their heads at each other when it's over. I see students in the Maple Hill hallway with their instruments, on their way to workshops or private lessons—places I'll never go if I can't get over my stage fright.

And I see Mami cleaning a big house and Papi driving a big truck. They work so hard so that I get to do something I love. Maybe it's time that I do something hard—something scary and terrifying and humiliating.

Ronny is right: I *have* to go back. The countdown started the Sunday after Thanksgiving.

I say, "The invitation . . . that was my 'final notice.'"

Ronny nods.

"Okay."

"Okay?"

"Yes." I march back into the orchestra closet and say, "I'll do it."

Mr. Newsum claps. "Most excellent," he says.

I snatch the sticky note from him and go directly to my locker. I get out my laptop and write the email—right there on the hallway floor.

Dear Ms. Williams,

Hello, this is Jo Ramos from Kennesaw Middle School. Thank you for inviting me to play for the residents again. Please let me know when the next performance will be so I can ask my parents.

Thank you again.

Josefina Ramos

P.S. Ronny said he would like to come too.

14

PROBABLY I AM A GENIUS

RONNY

A big city bus is stopping at the traffic light and people get off. Most of them look pretty tired like my mom but none of them are her. She did the food shopping after work and now me and Bianca are freezing our butts off waiting to help her carry stuff back to the apartment.

"Ants can lift up to fifty times their body weight," Bianca says. "They are the strongest insects alive."

"Yeah but they're so small so who cares."

"If you were as strong as an ant, you could lift a car."

My dad used to carry in all the food by himself before the forklift attacked him. Like he would bet me that he could do it all in one trip and he always would because his arms could carry anything. But then he had the back surgery and now the physical therapy doctor says he can do zero lifting. My dad saw the guy today for some special exercises but now he's laying down in lots of pain so is he really getting better?

"Yeah that would be pretty cool," I say.

This old Black lady gets off with some plastic food bags and

I'm pretty sure she lives across from us in another building. She drops a bag and a bunch of apples are going everywhere on the sidewalk so me and Bianca pick them up.

"Thank you," she says. She's got big glasses and a cool furry hat. "Not as strong as I used to be."

"If you were an ant you could carry a hundred bags," I say.

"Is that so?"

"It is so," Bianca says. "Maybe two hundred."

"Have to keep that in mind." The old lady looks at the Apartments way far away down the sidewalk. "You two wouldn't wanna give me a hand to my place, would ya?"

Bianca is taking three big steps back.

"Oh man," I say. "Come on stop."

"Honey—you okay?" the old lady says.

"Three steps back and run like the wind," I say. "It's what they tell us in school about Stranger Danger."

"My body is *mine mine mine*," Bianca says real low.

"That's one of the songs," I say. "They train us pretty good to be afraid of people we don't know."

"Honey, I'm Loretta," the old lady says. "I brought you that cherry pie when you moved in a while back. I'm sure you remember that."

Now Bianca is smiling. "Yeah. I do."

Loretta laughs and her face is turning into wrinkles like she's been laughing her whole life. "Never got a thank-you note, though."

"Ha yeah," I say. "Okay she's Bianca and I'm Ronny and I

thanked you by eating most of that pie." Now I'm grabbing her bags and give some to Bianca. "We just gotta be back to help my mom or she's gonna be mad."

"Fair enough," Loretta says. "And if you don't make it, I'll tell her you were helping an old lady with bad knees."

We go down the sidewalk past a big parking lot for all the shops. There's a bunch of places like the Dairy Queen and laundromat and the store where Jo's mom gets all her food and everything is in Spanish. This one called Zoe's Fellowship is like a church and in the summer they open the doors and you can hear them singing. A couple little shopping carts from the Dollar Store are spread out all over like people forgot to put them back.

"You do this by yourself all the time?" I say. "Wow that's crazy."

"Used to be that I'd walk a big loop around the whole complex every day," Loretta says. "These knees won't allow that anymore."

We're passing the basketball court and swings and man there's another shopping cart. It's shoved way into a bush and upside down like it's been there forever. Probably somebody should put them all at the bus stop for people to use for their food and stuff. We keep going and man my arms are burning. I'm looking way back at the traffic light to see if another bus is here but nothing yet. Loretta's building is right across from ours and finally we're at her front door putting the bags down.

"I'm sorry I tried to run away from you," Bianca says. "Thank you for the pie."

"You're welcome." Loretta is pulling something out of her purse and now she's giving me five bucks.

"Ha come on," I say. "No."

"Showing an old lady a measure of kindness is worth a few dollars."

It's not a lot okay but it's closer to $878 than zero dollars. "Yeah but you made us the pie."

Loretta is smiling weird. "Truth be told, I bought it at the store. It was on sale." She's covering her mouth and laughing now. "Then I took off the plastic and heated it up so it felt homemade."

"Hahahaha," I say and we're all laughing. "Oh man wow that was really smart."

"I wanted to make you one, but I just didn't have it in me that day." I'm trying to give her the money back but she won't take it. "Buy some ice cream or something," she says. "Maybe even a pie."

We all laugh some more and now me and Bianca are running back down the sidewalk. I got five bucks and tomorrow I'm probably getting a job at the Manor so things are getting better. Probably it's not gonna be enough to get rid of FINAL NOTICE but maybe we can pay some of it and they'll give us more time.

"Wait," I say when we're at the playground because that shopping cart is making my brain spin. It's still there all buried in the bushes and now I'm going over and pulling it out. Bianca helps me flip it over and I'm checking to see if it's broken.

"The front wheel looks funny," she says.

I take it to the sidewalk and try it out. "Kinda goes to one side but maybe it's okay."

"It's really squeaky."

"Yeah but it works and it can hold stuff."

"Whose is it?"

"I don't know it was just here. It's bigger than the Dollar Store ones so we're not stealing it or anything."

"Mom will probably be happy," Bianca says.

"Oh man not just Mom."

Way down at the light there's a bus stopping so we're running again. We keep passing people with lots of bags and I'm thinking about my idea to have a ton of shopping carts for people to use but now I have an idea that is a hundred times better.

"It's like a delivery cart," I say real loud because the cart makes a ton of noise on the sidewalk. "I'll carry stuff for people and they'll pay me."

"Why do you need money?"

"Get my Xbox fixed," I say because Bianca is a blabbermouth and will probably ruin it if I tell her about the car. "Plus maybe I'll get you a Christmas present if you stop being annoying."

"Mom and Dad won't let you go outside at night."

"Okay so I'll do it after school before it's dark," I say and man my legs are tired and my fingers are freezing. Way down I see my mom and she has a lot of bags in her hand. "Or on weekends when people go to Target and shop for . . . *CHRISTMAS PRESENTS OH MAN BIANCA ARE YOU GETTING THIS? PROBABLY I AM A GENIUS!*"

15

THE GIG

JO

RONNY and I watch the parent car line creep toward the auditorium pickup door. I see Mami's car at the back—the bright pink *Dream Clean* lettering glitters in the sun. We wanted to walk to the Manor, but our parents said it was too cold and the way there doesn't have any sidewalks.

"Yeah so if I get twenty bucks a day and more on the weekends I could make a lot," Ronny tells me. "My parents said Bianca has to come too when she's off the bus and I have to pay her in ice cream. And I can't take money from old people."

"How do you know if they're old?"

"Like if they walk slow or just look old."

I zip my coat up. "Did you tell your parents what the money is for?"

"Yeah my Xbox," he says. "Maybe some presents if there's extra and that's not really a lie okay."

Not *really*. "It's a very smart plan. I think you will make money."

"Yeah probably I'm a genius." He walks back and forth in front of the glass windows, nodding and drumming his hands on his chest. "And if this Sarah lady makes me change a hundred old people diapers a day I'll do it. Like they could make me the main diaper person and everybody at school will be like 'Why is Ronny always smelling like diapers?' but who cares because I'll be getting lots of money."

Part of me wishes I was changing diapers.

But the rest of me knows exactly what I need to do.

I say, "I'm glad you're going to be there."

"Yeah probably I should be your cello assistant all the time. Like give you water and hold a fan in front of your face when you're melting."

I picture it—Ronny walking into my audition with me. I imagine us going to class together on my first day at Maple Hill, when I don't know anyone. Thinking about him there makes it all seem less scary. "I wish you played the cello too."

"Ha come on I can't even sing good."

I say, "You could come with me."

Ronny's smile turns into a blank stare out the window. He brushes the hair out of his eyes and digs in his backpack for his winter hat. "Yeah but Ms. Q would miss me and all my amazing jokes. Plus there's a singing cat situation with Bri happening and probably I'm gonna want to see where that goes so yeah."

"I know—"

"Your mom's here," he says, and walks out to the car line.

Mami drives us out of the parking lot and down the windy hill behind school. Ronny jokes with her about wanting boiled donkey for dinner, but mostly he stares out the window. Something is wrong—he's terrible at pretending to be okay. Is he just thinking about the money? Or was it what I said about him coming to Maple Hill?

At the stop sign, Mami turns right onto the highway and then pulls into the Manor. She walks in with us to meet Ms. Sarah, and they talk by the front desk for a few minutes.

"Oh, the pleasure is ours," Ms. Sarah tells Mami. "We're glad to have her back. You too, Ronny. I talked to your dad today on the phone, and he said your gram spent some great years here."

"Yeah she loved all those little finches you have in the back." He looks around. "Where's everybody at?"

"Afternoon naps," Ms. Sarah whispers. "They'll be waking up soon. Perfect timing for you two."

"Oh man," Ronny whispers to me. "Diaper time."

Mami gives me a hug. "Buena suerte, mijita. I'll see you at home."

"Shall we?" Ms. Sarah asks when Mami is gone.

"Let's do it," Ronny says.

She leads us down the hallway to the skinny office where I played *Arioso*. Inside, two nurses type on computers and look at charts. Ms. Sarah walks past them to a door at the back I didn't notice last Friday. It has a cot, a sink, and a small table in the corner.

And a music stand.

"Not bad, huh?" she says. "Your own little practice room studio."

I say, "You want me to play in here?"

"I want you to *start* here."

I look at Ronny. He shrugs. "So you don't want me to perform?" I ask.

Ms. Sarah takes a phone off the table and puts it on the bed. "None of the residents got to hear the real you on Friday. We're gonna change that." She picks up the receiver and hits a button. "Testing, testing, testing," she says.

I hear her voice from somewhere else—outside the little room. I peek my head out into the office, and look up at a speaker in the ceiling.

It's an intercom.

I say, "They can hear, but not see me."

"*Exactly.*" She hangs up the phone. "I was hoping you'd be free twice a week after school to play for the dinner hour— somewhere in the three to five range. We eat a *little* earlier here, you know. If you could do three days a week that would be even better, but I'm guessing you have sports or music after school."

"Haha sports," Ronny says. "We don't do sports."

"Just string ensemble on Monday and cello lessons on Thursday," I say.

"Perfect. So how about: Tuesday, Wednesday, and Friday right after school until four fifteen. Both your parents said you were allowed to ride the city bus home afterward."

"Yeah if we're with somebody and it's not dark," Ronny tells her. "The Apartments are like a mile from here."

"And there's a stop right across the street." Ms. Sarah shuffles through papers on her clipboard and pulls out a bus schedule. "Route 55 has a bus there every day at four thirty. That should be perfect."

"Thank you, so much." I think about what Ronny said—how this is my OPERATION FINAL NOTICE too. "But how is playing in this room—alone—going to help me with my stage fright?"

"Glad you asked." Ms. Sarah looks at a calendar on her clipboard. "On Friday, you'll perform live in the Lounge for the residents—plus Wednesday the twenty-third for the holiday party with their families. That's a total of three mini concerts."

A few bees buzz around my stomach. "Three."

She holds up three fingers. "Three."

Ronny fills up a paper cup near the sink and gulps down a mouthful of water. "So what am I doing?"

"You're going to do what you did last Friday."

"Haha so sell candy?"

Ms. Sarah smiles like she has a secret. "Not quite."

We follow her back to the hallway and walk down to the cafe. Workers dressed in all white wipe down tables and refill cups at the juice station.

"Do you see any family members joining them for a meal?" Ms. Sarah asks us.

I look at each table—only residents. "No."

"Yeah but it's so early," Ronny says. "People are at work and stuff."

"Correct," Ms. Sarah says. "Their families are busy, living their busy lives."

More residents slowly walk down the hallway and find tables. Most of them sit with another person, but others are alone.

"On the weekends it's not much different," she tells us. "Sunday lunch? That's crowded. The after-church crowd is bustling. But the rest of the week is like this. Quiet, yes. But lonely."

"So like you want me to hang out with them?" Ronny asks.

"Exactly. They absolutely loved you last week—I've never seen them laugh so hard." Ms. Sarah holds up a finger. "But listen too. Get to know them. Play a game of checkers or gin rummy. Just *be* with them. It's good for their minds and spirits. Good for yours as well."

"Okay so hang out and don't sell them candy," Ronny says. "I can do that."

"Now: Let's talk money."

Ronny's eyes go very wide. "Yeah let's."

Ms. Sarah consults her clipboard again. "Each year, we get a community event budget. If I don't spend it all, the board of directors will just subtract it from next year's budget. Can't have that, can we?"

"No we cannot," Ronny says. "Like really that would be very not good."

"So: We'll pay for your bus passes—and of course you can both have as much food as you like—"

"And juice," Ronny says.

"And juice." Ms. Sarah runs her pencil down a sheet of paper. "How does five hundred dollars for the whole month sound, between the two of you?"

Ronny's jaw hangs open.

I say, "Wow."

"Oh, I think it will be worth every penny," Ms. Sarah says. "For the residents *and* you two."

"That's good. That's really good," Ronny says. His eyes dart back and forth. He's probably thinking about the rest of the money. "Ms. Sarah, I have to say you are probably a Christmas hero."

"Will it be enough to buy a new Xbox?" she asks. "I know how expensive they can be."

Ronny stares. "Uh."

"Your dad said your old one broke. And hey—that shopping cart business he mentioned is pretty smart."

"Ha yeah," Ronny says. He looks at me for one second. "Yeah."

Ms. Sarah checks her watch. "Everybody good to start today?" We both nod. "You're on the clock, then. Head to your stations, and come find me if there's any problems."

When she's gone, Ronny grabs me by the shoulders. "Jo—"

"Yes?"

"I need to borrow two hundred and fifty dollars from you."

I nod without thinking.

He hugs me so hard, I can't breathe. "I mean I'll pay you back okay I promise. I'll cart around people's stuff every day after school or maybe find senior citizens who don't have diabetes to buy my candy and I'll get you back your half—"

"You don't have to pay me back," I say. Wasn't what he did last Friday for me worth a thousand dollars?

I hug him this time, just as hard. My eyes burn around the edges. Who will do that for me at Maple Hill next year? What if there's only one Ronny in the world, and he goes to Kennesaw?

I say, "You can have it all."

"Okay yeah yeah." He laughs. "Ha okay good luck playing today. I'm gonna go talk to old people."

"Residents."

"Yeah residents ha."

I walk back to my new practice room and tune my cello. After warming up, I turn on the intercom like Ms. Sarah showed me. I play the piece they should have gotten to hear on Friday: *Arioso*.

It feels weird at first. I think about notes coming out of every speaker in the building, every person being able to hear me. But then it feels just like my room at home—no one in here but me. Halfway through the piece I don't even notice the intercom.

When I'm done, the two nurses in the office area clap. My heart beats steadily, and sweat doesn't drip off me. I'm warm all over in a good way—like a torch burning up every single angry bee.

This is my mission—and I accept it.

16

MEAN NOREEN

RONNY

"YOU say it like 'catsup,'" Carl says on Wednesday. He's moving the checker piece real slow and his hand is shaking pretty bad but he's still kicking my butt. Yesterday we played a bunch and I barely won any games. "The *cats* are *up.*"

"You mean ketchup?" I say.

"Catsup."

"That's how people used to say it?"

"Everyone used to say it like that."

I eat some vanilla pudding and probably it's my fourth cup. Carl says it's sugar free but who cares it's still good. "Like when did it change?"

"Hard to say," he says. "Maybe it was always that way, and we never knew."

"Catsup."

"That's the one."

"Sounds weird," I say.

"A lot of things from back then seem weird."

"Ha yeah like horses did stuff that cars do today."

He laughs real loud. The cafe is pretty full and Jo's cello is pumping through the PA system. It's like a radio or something which is good because one day she'll probably be on the radio when she's famous.

"She's something special," Carl says. "Isn't she?"

"Yeah she's gonna be a professional one day."

Carl double jumps me. "King me, young man."

"Oh man." I give him the checker and he's trying to stack it to make the king. But he can't get it on the top right so I do it for him. "Probably you could be a professional too if they had that for checkers."

He laughs but now he's coughing a little. "You should ease up on that pudding."

I'm scooping out a big spoonful and eating it. "Why?"

"They put medicine in it," he says real quiet. "To help us go the bathroom."

"Ha oh man really?"

His face turns into all wrinkles as he laughs. "I'm joking."

"Good one," I say but don't finish the pudding just in case.

There's a really high-pitch sneeze that comes through the intercom and I look at the ceiling. "Bless you," I say and then Jo keeps playing. "Okay I'm gonna go talk to some other people and probably read a book on how to get better at checkers."

"*Catsup* with you later," he says and goes to sit with these two ladies.

I go to the drink machine and get some juice. Every table

has two people so that's good because nobody is lonely. Now I'm seeing a big round table at the back with one lady just staring at her food real close. She's in a wheelchair and has an oxygen tank thing so I'm pretty sure she's the mean-face lady named Noreen.

"This girl Bri at my school thinks her cat can sing," I say and I'm sitting next to her. "I kinda want to believe it too because that would be like a miracle or something but also I think she should see a doctor."

The lady is doing her really mean face at me. "You should know something about me."

"Okay."

"I don't like children."

"Yeah tell me about it," I say. "I got a little sister and pretty much her job is being annoying."

Now Noreen is making that mean face at her food. Probably that is just her normal face? "This is cold."

"Like it's not hot enough?"

"Stone cold." She's looking up at me with these really small eyes that are like angry black beans. "Why would anyone serve me *stone-cold* food?"

"I don't know."

"Richard would *never* serve me this. I won't eat it."

"Okay," I say but who is Richard?

We're just sitting there listening to Jo's cello for a while. Man she's good so how can this plan not work?

"But I have to eat it," Noreen says.

"Like they make you?"

"I can't take my *pills* if I don't *eat*."

"Oh yeah my gram took a lot of pills when she was here. Wait did you know her? Her first name was Clementine but everybody here called her Old Clemmie. She died a couple years ago."

"I didn't know her." Noreen is shaking her head. "And I won't eat cold food."

I look around for a kitchen person or nurse or Sarah but everybody is busy. "Okay I'll go ask somebody."

I get her plate and now I'm at the food counter waving at this lady doing dishes in the back.

"You need something?" she says.

"Yeah can you heat this up?"

She comes out and takes the plate. "Mean Noreen ask you to do this?"

"Ha yeah," I say and is that what they call her? Okay so it's pretty true but still kind of mean. "She says it's stone cold and won't eat it but has to because of her pills."

The kitchen lady microwaves it and brings it back to me with all this steam rising up from it. Like I can hear stuff sizzling all around inside so definitely not cold anymore.

"Thanks," I say and go back to Noreen's table. "Okay so the kitchen lady heated this up really hot for you."

She sticks her fork into it and a bunch of steam goes in her face. "*This* will burn the skin off the roof of my mouth."

"Yeah probably let it cool down," I say. "My mom gets these

95

frozen pizza pocket things and they always get like lava in the middle when you microwave them so you should probably wait."

"I won't eat this."

"Yeah but your pills."

She's pushing the plate at me. "Richard would never do such a thing."

"Yeah but it will be okay to eat in like a couple minutes."

Now she's shaking her head. "They send a child to burn my food."

"I mean I'll be thirteen in May."

"A child—to ruin my dinner."

I get a spoon from the next table and dig in her potatoes to see if they're still hot. "I think you can almost eat them."

"*Excuse* me." Noreen is grabbing the plate but she can't reach it so she just keeps trying until I push it back to her. "This is *my* dinner."

"Ha," I say and now Jo is coming over with her cello stuff all ready to go.

"The bus will be here soon," she says.

"Okay bye Noreen." I stand up and she's saying something real low and giving me and the hot steaming potatoes a mean face. "I'll see you on Friday and sorry about burning your food."

"I don't appreciate this sort of treatment," she says to us but I'm walking away pretty fast. "And neither would Richard."

"Who's Richard?" Jo says.

"I don't know but he's way better at stuff than me."

We say bye to Sarah and now we're crossing the highway at the light to the bus stop on the other side. It's pretty cold out with tons of clouds like maybe snow is in our future.

"How did I sound?" Jo says.

"Oh yeah awesome like yesterday. You're getting good playing into a phone. Was it still weird?"

"A little. I forgot I even had an audience for a few minutes." She's getting our bus passes out of her jacket and giving me one. "How was the cafe?"

"Pretty good except for Noreen. I'm still bad at checkers and did you know they used to call ketchup *catsup*?"

Our bus comes and it's like half-full so we get two seats in the back part near this guy with a ton of grocery bags. There's a big food store next to the Manor so probably a lot of people coming home this time could use my cart services.

"Okay so OPERATION FINAL NOTICE is happening," I say. "But like what is your plan for the Friday concert?"

"Mr. Newsum and I are going to work on that tomorrow at my lesson." Jo is hugging her cello real close and oh man she's scared. "I just need to get over it."

"Yeah just roll right over it."

"Uh-huh."

"Just Carlos Prieto this thing and crush it."

"Yes," she says but not like she really thinks she can do it.

"Like destroy it Ms. Q-style when she goes after her peanut butter crackers."

Jo is taking in this giant breath and lets it out real slow. "Just like that."

17

THE QUESTION

JO

MR. NEWSUM waves his hand to cut me off.

"What about hanging on that A longer?" he asks. "Like *daa dah dahhhh dah dah dah dah dah dah dahhhhhhhhhhhhhhhhh.*" He plays the phrase on his cello. "Hear it?"

I say, "Draw it out *more?*"

"Try it."

I mark the measure on my music. We've been working on the Bach D Minor prelude for most of the lesson. Not the notes, but the phrasing—how the measures fit together with different volumes and emphasis.

I start the section over. When I get to the climax, I stretch out the note so long it sounds like I will never resolve the phrase with the next arpeggio. But then, right as I'm about to run out of bow room, I plunge down into the next measure with so much volume, the bass vibrates in my chest.

"*Ha!*" Mr. Newsum says. "Took me right to the cliff edge, you did. Bravo."

He was right. The sound has more danger and beauty than before—deeper, like I dug down into something I didn't even know was there.

I ask, "Will the string faculty mind that I'm adding my own flair?"

"They'll be impressed," he says. "They expect you to have the skill and intonation. But make it *interesting?* That will get their attention."

The clock in the orchestra closet says 3:45 p.m. Mami will be here to pick me up in fifteen minutes.

"Okay, enough Bach," Mr. Newsum says. "Let's talk mental state: How are you feeling about tomorrow?"

I stretch my neck from side to side. "Very nervous."

"Honesty is good."

"But also determined. I don't want to do it, but I know I have to."

"Excellent." He puts his cello back in the case and grabs two pieces of paper from his desk. He gives one to me. "I've been compiling this all week from my old undergrad classes and a healthy amount of YouTube. Lots of professional musicians bravely sharing their stage fright on there, let me tell you. I had it pretty good myself, though I usually got dizzy instead of overheating."

I say, "Really?"

"Oh yeah. But us bassists never got much solo time, so it wasn't an issue I had to confront as often."

I read the worksheet. At the top it says *Jo-Jo Ma's Performance*

Anxiety Management Plan. Below, I see a short list in large, bold font.

Prep for It

Admit It

Breathe Through It

Use It

"There were nine," Mr. Newsum tells me. "Practicing in front of people, for example, which we're doing. Also being prepared—which you already are." He pulls his curly hair into a ponytail on the top of his head. "There was one about eating a banana because the potassium apparently calms you down, but I couldn't confirm it."

"How about one for uncontrollable sweating," I say.

"Actually, that's number one: You need to *prep* for your fear sweats."

Esther already told me that. "Wear lighter clothes and a sweatband."

He nods. "And right before you play tomorrow, walk outside in the freezing cold for twenty seconds. Just long enough to cool off."

I scribble that down. "What does 'admit it' mean?"

"That one really struck me." Mr. Newsum leans back in his chair. "Apparently we can get nervous about *being* nervous. But *admitting* that you're nervous can be quite calming. Don't pretend, just say to yourself what's true: *I'm experiencing stage fright.* Try it."

I say, "I am experiencing stage fright."

"Weird—I know."

I read number three again: *Breathe Through It*. "I have been doing the two in and four out exercises."

"Good. I read about another useful one, just for the moment of panic. Watch." Mr. Newsum sniffs air through his nose as hard as he can—a one-second, nose-crinkling sniffle. "When we get that nervous, we often forget to breathe. This injects air right to the brain and disrupts the anxiety."

I try it.

"Again," he says. "Imagine you're trying to suck in all the oxygen in the entire room through your nose."

I sniffle again, hard enough to burn my nostrils.

"Now we're talking." Mr. Newsum studies the paper. "Saved the hardest for last: You need to find a way to convert this stage fright into something useful."

"How do I do that?"

He folds his arms. "I listened to a podcast with a concert violinist yesterday—fascinating insight. She described her stage fright as a fiery ball of hot lava burning in her chest. What does it feel like for you?"

I say, "Bees."

"Bees?"

I nod. "A hive of angry bees."

"Oh, Jo." Mr. Newsum leans his head to one side. "I'm so sorry. That sounds really terrible."

"It is." But it feels good to tell him—*amazing*, actually. Every time I say it out loud, it's less scary somehow. "I don't want to be scared anymore. I just want to play."

"Mmm." He nods, and then taps the paper. "So this ball

of lava inside her—beehive, etc.—she decides one day to think of it *not* as a ball of lava, but as *the sun*. And instead of burning her up inside, she will warm the audience with her music. A tremendous perspective change, I thought."

I put my chair back in the band room next door. I picture all the angry bees getting out of my hive and stinging the residents—the whole room running around screaming.

I say, "Thanks for looking this up. I'm going to try to use them tomorrow."

"You're very welcome." He sighs. "Here's the deal, Jo: These strategies are great, but they're just Band-Aids. There's another layer to this you need to think about here. Esther was kidding when she said it, I think, but she was onto something."

"What?"

He looks at me very closely. "Why do you love cello?"

I don't even have to think. "Because it's the most beautiful sound in the whole world."

He smiles. "So why wouldn't you want other people to hear it too?"

18

BIG GIANT CART PROBLEMS

RONNY

"THAT looks pretty heavy," I say.

I'm way down at another apartment building and this guy is taking a giant bag of salt out of his trunk. He's got a nice suit and shoes so probably he doesn't want to get them dirty. "For the snow coming next week."

"I mean I can help you."

"My door's right there. I'll be okay."

"Yeah but this cart would be better."

He's trying real hard to lift it like when my dad tries to carry heavy stuff now but can't. "Yeah, it would," he says. "Thanks."

We put it in the cart together and now I'm wheeling it to his door like fifty feet away. He has to pull the front to guide it 'cause it's really heavy and that one bad wheel is going crooked.

"You're really getting into the spirit of Christmas," he says. "Thanks again."

"Ha yeah," I say but he shuts the door before I can tell him about giving me money for helping.

"You need a sign," Bianca says. She's on the sidewalk looking out for other people who maybe need me. "To tell people that there is a fee."

"Probably yeah."

"Dad said dinner is in twenty minutes."

It's getting pretty close to dark. "Okay just gonna go to the bus stop one more time. How much did we make?"

"Eight dollars." Bianca gives me the wallet and I count it. "Better than nothing."

"Yeah but not enough."

These headlights shine on us for a second and now I'm seeing a big red tow truck go by real slow. It says *Vince's Towing* in gold letters on the side and this huge white guy with a big black beard is driving. Now he's backing up so he's right behind a blue car, like parked butt to butt.

This metal cross thing way high up on the tow truck is coming down and now it slides under the blue car. The big bearded guy jumps out and checks something and presses a button and the metal cross lifts the whole back of the blue car up. Now he gets back in his truck and is driving away real slow with the car behind him.

"*Hey!*" a lady yells and oh man she's running after the blue car so fast. But she's got a bathrobe over her pajamas and it's flying around like a cape and the tow truck guy speeds up so there's no way she catches him. She keeps screaming and now there's a guy running out to her and they're yelling at each other and she screams a couple bad words right in a row and is she crying? "*I paid, Repo Man!*" she yells.

"He just took it," Bianca says and the guy is trying to get the lady back inside now. "Why did he do that?"

"Oh man," I say and it's like ice in my stomach. My brain is spinning on *Repo Man*. "Repossession."

"What's that?"

"They didn't pay their car bill," I say and what if that lady needs it for work because she's a nurse or has a cleaning company like Jo's mom? The guy is finally getting her inside now but a bunch of people are watching and oh man is that going to happen to us?

"I'm gonna do one more," I say because no way is *Vince's Towing* taking my mom's car like that.

"But Dad said—"

"Just tell him I'm fixing the wheel and I'll be there in like ten minutes."

"Don't you need help steering?"

"No I got it," I say and I'm running like crazy to the bus stop.

A couple people get off but nobody is carrying stuff. Okay wait now these two Black ladies with some bags are coming down and I roll over to them. They got the same cool puffy jackets on but one is pink and the other is like a shiny blue.

"Hi I'm Ronny," I say. "I'm helping people carry their stuff to their apartments for the holidays."

"That so?" the taller one says. She's got really long eyelashes and big earrings. "Spreading a little Christmas cheer?"

"Yeah but I'm doing it for money too."

Now they're laughing. "Okay, okay," says the other. She's

way shorter than her friend and has this big giant smile as her regular face like everything is funny. "How much?"

"Five bucks."

"That's fair," she says. "My back about to be thrown out."

They put their stuff in and now I'm rolling after them. It's pretty hard to keep the cart straight because these bags are so heavy and is the wheel getting worse? I look real quick in the bags and it's milk and soup and some eggs probably for the storm coming that other guy was talking about. Oh man the cart is really swerving and now I'm pushing real hard on the one side so it doesn't fly off the sidewalk.

"You okay?" the tall one asks.

"Ha yeah good."

I've never been on this side of the Apartments before and it's like downhill or something because I'm going faster now. I pull back but the cart just goes to the left on the bad wheel so I'm pushing and pulling to keep it straight. Probably this is how Jo feels onstage because I am sweating so much under my coat.

Now the ladies are turning around to say something but the cart is so loud I can't hear it and are they pointing at something? All the milk is sliding to the front so it's even harder now to control and probably I should put brakes on this thing. One of them slips and almost falls but her friend catches her and they're laughing and pointing again and now I get that they were trying to tell me about *ice*.

Oh man I'm pulling back real hard but too late the front

wheels are already sliding and now the back wheels and I'm slipping. I hit the ground and get dragged on my butt for a couple feet but now it's pavement again and I get all twisted and have to let go of the handle.

"*Hey!*" I say but they're still laughing about the falling thing so now I'm shouting louder and they look back and jump out of the way at the last second. The cart flies by them and goes *boom* into a light post which knocks it over and all their stuff is flying out on the sidewalk.

"Oh man," I say and run down to it and it's bad real bad. The milk is mostly okay except for one bottle spilling everywhere but nope there's another broken one and I'm picking up egg containers and yeah they're mostly broken. "Oh man that's a lot of eggs."

"Boy—you almost killed me!" the tall lady says.

The short one is picking up stuff too but she's still sort of smiling at the whole thing. "I told ya to watch it. Didn't you hear me?"

"Probably this would never happen to the ants," I say.

"What now?"

"I'm really sorry."

We pick it all up and yeah everything is covered in milk. The short lady finds like two okay jugs of milk but the rest is ruined.

"So you don't have to pay me," I say. "Probably I should pay you."

"That's right you're gonna pay us," the tall one says.

"Should make you ride back to the Target right now and buy it yourself."

"I got some money."

"How much?"

I count all the dollar bills from Loretta and the two other people today and my failed candy bake sale thing. "Seventeen bucks."

She's looking at her friend and shaking her head. "Guess it'll have to be enough."

I'm holding out the money and she's trying to take it but why can't I let go? Those big snowmen guys are doing sumo wrestling in my stomach and I think about Vince and his giant metal cross driving around the Apartments looking for us.

"Kid," she says and she's tugging real hard. "Let go."

"Sorry," I say and now I'm running back up the sidewalk. I'm pulling the cart by the front so the bad wheel doesn't wreck everything again and my hands are freezing. By the playground I slip on another icy part and the cart smashes into another light post messing up the bad wheel even more. Pretty much I'm dragging it the rest of the way home and is this how adults throw their back out? There's these bushes behind our building and I'm shoving it in there but it won't go.

Now I'm stomping on it with the bottom of my foot so hard the cage part is bending and I keep stomping and kicking until I can barely breathe.

19

THE CRAMP

JO

"ARE you sick?" Ronny asks me.

"No."

"You keep sniffling like you're sick."

I push the drink machine button and fill my cup with juice. "It's a breathing technique Mr. Newsum taught me."

Ronny waves at one of the residents, then goes back to frowning—his face for most of the day. He said there's something wrong with the cart and he might need to find another one.

I say, "I'm supposed to be honest about feeling nervous."

"Yeah so are you feeling nervous?"

"Extremely."

He points to my stomach. "Bees?"

"Bees," I say.

But I'm also tired. Mr. Newsum's question kept me up last night—I couldn't stop thinking about it. I *do* love the cello, and it *is* the most beautiful sound in the world. I want people to hear it—but there's other cellists out there.

Why do they have to hear it from *me?*

Ronny gets a cup of raisins from the snack bar and we sit down. He dumps the whole thing in his mouth. "Yeah actually I'm nervous for you too," he says.

"Why?"

"I mean it's pretty hard to watch somebody doing something really embarrassing."

"Oh—*thanks.*"

"No no like you're my friend and it's not good if you're having a hard time so I'm saying it's hard for me too. Listen you're gonna do amazing okay because how would it get worse?"

I'm trying *not* to think about that. "It won't."

"Maybe if you fainted or something and fell over," Ronny says. "Like if you knocked yourself out with your own cello okay yeah that would be worse. I mean I'd try to catch you. Probably I should sit in the front row just in case."

I say, "If that happens, catch the cello."

I finish my juice and go back to the practice room. I keep looking at the wall clock, counting the seconds until five. With fifteen minutes left, I change into gym shorts and my favorite cello T-shirt—a cello saying to a double bass *You had me at* cello, which I got at string camp last summer. After that, I walk outside for a freezing cold minute until I'm almost shaking.

At 4:55 p.m., Ms. Sarah comes to get me.

"Almost showtime." She grabs my music stand. "Ready?"

The beehive buzzes. I pull in a sharp nose breath. "Ready."

Residents fill every seat in the Lounge. Are there more people here than last Friday? I follow Ms. Sarah to the front and set up in the chair. Ronny sits just a few feet away in the front row. He does a catching motion with both arms. I wipe sweat off my forehead with the armband Esther gave me.

"Okay, residents," Ms. Sarah says. "We are once again very, very lucky to have with us the talented Josefina Ramos, who as you know has been providing our dinner soundtrack. As you may recall, she is a member of the highly decorated Kennesaw Orchestra—"

"And string ensemble," Ronny says. "That's like all the best kids from orchestra."

"And the string ensemble," Ms. Sarah says. "She will be playing some lovely music for us the next few weeks—including the holiday party before Christmas. Aren't we so lucky?"

They smile and nod. I hear Ronny say "I mean we're getting paid" to the resident next to him—Noreen. She fiddles with the tube running from her nose down to the oxygen tank and glares at him.

Now she glares at me.

"Let's give her another warm Manor welcome," Ms. Sarah says.

They clap. The room goes silent.

I close my eyes and take in a deep breath for two counts. Exhale for four.

I am nervous.

It is normal to be nervous when performing.

I can feel the beehive vibrating all the way up to my ears. I try to imagine doing something helpful with it. But all I want is for it to be out of me—to throw it a thousand miles from here.

I open my eyes and see the opening measure of *Arioso*.

I count myself in.

One and

Two and

Ready and

Go.

My down bow hits the string too hard. The sound breaks the air like thunder, booming out of key. For one second, I panic—but then I pull in a sharp sniffle so hard, my nose burns. The distraction works, and my fingers find the right positions and muscle memory takes over. I'm hot—but not on fire. Gym clothes to the rescue.

I concentrate on every single note and finger position and drive the bow with force. Am I playing faster than normal? It's definitely more dramatic—I'm overdoing the vibrato, but with good intonation.

But I'm doing it.

I'm playing well, onstage.

And then suddenly I'm headed toward the end. The notes run down the neck, my hand spanning strings for the final sequence that repeats the opening melody. My bow drags across the final notes. The sound hangs in the air for a few seconds, and then disappears.

It's over.

Ronny jumps out of his seat and shouts, "*Whoooooooooooooooooooooooooooooooo!*"

The residents clap. I smile—I think I could float to the ceiling. Tears build at the corners of my eyes.

Ms. Sarah gives me two thumbs-up.

I did it.

"Yeah you're crushing it," Ronny whispers. He leans forward in his seat and hands me a bottle of water. I take three big sips. "Oh man are you crying?"

I shake my head and wipe my eyes. My hands shake. "I'm okay."

"Ha you're amazing. Okay water break over."

He leans back and I take a few deep breaths. I feel only a faraway buzzing in my stomach. Did the music put the hive to sleep? I get out the D Minor prelude. The hand positions are a little more technical, but nothing to worry about. Then I'll finish with G Major prelude and be done. I am definitely going to need a shower tonight.

I set my fingers, then count myself in.

One and

Two and

Ready and

Go.

Pain shoots across the top of my left hand in the third

measure. I try to relax my grip on the strings, but my wrist won't obey. I play slower during a melody that walks down the scale in single, even notes. But I have to bridge a large gap in the next phrase that leads me right to a double stop—drawing the bow across two strings at the same time. I hear the intonation sliding off key, so I focus on each note to get the right pitch but—

"*Ah!*" I scream.

I stare at my left hand. It's clamped to the cello neck—it won't move.

Cramp.

A *cramp?* I haven't had a cramp since the first month I learned how to play.

This can't be happening.

I look at the audience. They stare back at me, eyes wide.

I use all my arm muscles to pull my wrist off. The pain gets worse—I almost scream again. But then the muscles relax.

And the cello slips.

I can't grab it.

Ronny jumps out of his seat to catch it, but he trips on Noreen's oxygen tank. He falls face-first into the cello, slamming his head on the curved edge of the lower bout. *Thunk* goes his skull against the wood. It knocks the whole instrument back toward me just enough so I can hook my arm under the neck and keep it from hitting the ground.

"Ohhhhh," Ronny groans. He blinks and yawns at the same time. His left cheekbone is already puffy. "*My face.*"

I ask, "Are you okay?"

"She can't breathe," a resident says.

A nurse runs over and puts the oxygen tube back in Noreen's nose.

"He tried . . . to kill me," Noreen gasps. She points a finger at Ronny. *That child tried to kill me.*"

20

CHRISTMAS IS MAYBE CANCELED

RONNY

"WHOA," Bianca says. "Your eye."

"I head-butted a cello." I throw my stuff down on the table and now I'm getting an ice pack from the freezer. The one Sarah gave me isn't cold anymore plus it smelled like weird soap. "Yeah also I almost suffocated a senior citizen, so it was a crazy night."

"Is your face broken?"

"Nurse Monica says probably not."

"Can you see?" Bianca says and she's holding up three fingers. "How many?"

"Seven."

"Mom is gonna be upset. She hates head injuries."

"It's not a head injury." I sit at the table and am moving my jaw up and down. It's like somebody hit me in the head with a cello-sized baseball bat. "It's a face injury. Probably my face is harder than spaceship metal okay, like nothing can hurt my face."

Way in the back bedroom we hear my dad talking real loud with somebody on the phone.

You don't—I will not—transferred—

It goes real quiet for like a minute and now he's coming in the kitchen all mad like whoever was on the phone was a big jerk. "Hey bud. How was—*BUDDY—WHAT—?*"

"I fell on Jo's cello," I say. "Yeah it was face-first but I'm okay. A bunch of nurses checked it out. Also the cello is good too we're pretty sure."

"Buddy—that looks *bad*." He gets another ice pack from the freezer. "I'm gonna call Mom."

"They already did," I say. "The lady in charge at the Manor called her and then I talked to her. They gave me Advil and ice."

"Oh buddy."

"How does a person fall face-first on a cello?" Bianca says.

I tell them the story and my dad keeps swapping out my ice packs and getting me more water.

"So really I saved her cello," I say. "With my face. Yeah and that thing is made out of maple wood so basically I ran into a tree is what happened. I'm a superhero and my power is deflecting hard stuff with my head."

Bianca is pretty much crying, she's laughing so hard. "This would only happen to you."

"I actually thought I broke her cello, which would be really bad because cellos are expensive and she needs it for her big audition."

"What big audition?" my dad says.

"To get in that music school. That's why she's playing at the Manor all these times."

Bianca is frowning pretty big. "She's leaving?"

"Not like America," I say. "Just maybe our school."

"Will she still come over?"

I make a face and, man, that hurts my cheek. "She's not *moving* okay jeez. She's just going to a new school."

My dad is trying to give me a new ice pack again. "I'm sorry, bud."

Now I'm getting the heck out of here and going to my room. "The cello hero needs sleep so please no more ice or water."

"Mom's gonna be home soon with pizza."

"Not hungry."

I put on sleeping shorts and shut off the lights before going up to my bed. Man, my face hurts and Nurse Monica said it would hurt way more later which is great just great. Jo felt so bad but really it was okay because wow if her cello broke that would be mission over. Actually maybe that would be good because then she'd have to stay at Kennesaw and everything would be the same. Like I know she can't really do that because she's the next Carlos Prieto but Maple Hill is taking her away just like the bank took our house.

The ice pack is leaking stuff all over my face. I wipe it off and now I'm looking out the window at our old house. The light way up in my old room is on and is that the kid in the window? Probably he's not eating leftover hospital cafeteria pizza his mom brings home on Fridays but the real stuff like what we used to get from the place next to the post office. I wonder if he did anything weird to my room like put all his sports trophies on the wall where my dad made that Nerf gun target.

I hear my mom come in the kitchen and lay down real quick. She talks to my dad and now she's coming in my room and says stuff but I'm a pretty good fake sleeper. She kisses my forehead and then I'm asleep for real dreaming about hospital pizza.

I wake up and rub my face but why does it hurt so bad? I remember everything real fast and see the desk clock blinking 12:32 a.m. I'm starving so I go to the kitchen and look for some pizza. There's a plate in the fridge with a note from my mom that just says *Cheese* and I'm so hungry I don't even heat it up. I have to chew on the one side because the other one hurts but man it's good even for hospital pizza.

Now I hear my parents whisper-yelling in their room. Like I'm not even trying to listen but the doors in this place block zero sounds so when I go back to my room I can pretty much hear everything by just standing there.

Dad: *I won't be one of those parents.*

Mom: *They will have a few stocking stuffers I got in the summer.*

Dad: *It's not the same.*

Mom: *Nothing is the same, Mark. We're improvising. We're rolling with the punches.*

Dad: *Skipping one therapy session isn't a big deal—I'll do the exercises at home. Then we can get them something better.*

Mom: Better would be you going back to work.

It goes real quiet.

Dad: I will not—

Mom: Do NOT raise your voice at me—

Lots more quiet. My stomach feels like a thousand degrees below zero. Pretty much I don't remember them ever fighting before we moved here and now they're yelling at each other about Christmas presents so what gives? I need to crush OPERATION FINAL NOTICE or things are gonna get way worse, but is that even possible?

I shut my door real quiet and check on Bianca. She's got like five covers on so I take two off because she's pretty sweaty. I climb up to my bunk and now I'm lying there for a while and listening to a big truck go by on the street outside. I don't remember hearing the traffic up in my old room. Was it always this loud? Probably that kid in my room is sleeping pretty good and his parents aren't whisper-yelling in their room about bills and back problems.

"Ronny," Bianca says real sleepy.

"Yeah."

"Santa isn't coming this year."

I'm thinking for a while because what do you say to that? "Yeah I don't think so."

"He's not even real."

I lean over so I'm looking at her. "I wasn't actually sure where you were on that so I wasn't gonna say anything."

Bianca yawns and now I think maybe she went back to sleep but then she's talking again. "Are we poor?"

"What?"

"Charlotte Finley said she lives across from all the poor people and we live across from her."

"Yeah Charlotte Finley needs to shut her big yap."

"But she's right."

"Come on we have stuff," I say. "Mom has a job and we have a car."

Oh man, for now we do.

"But we used to have another car," Bianca says. "And our own house."

"Yeah."

She goes to the bathroom and I'm remembering that really weird day when they told us we were moving. We were all in the living room and my dad wouldn't really talk much or look at us and my mom said a bunch of words about making some changes to save money. She was trying to smile and be all happy that we could stay in the same school and be with our friends but come on you could tell she was sad too. Pretty much right after that the bank put that stupid orange sticker on our house and we had those awkward garage sales where everybody bought our stuff. Oh man Mason came to one with his mom but they left when they saw it was our house.

"What are you really doing with all your money?" Bianca says when she comes back.

Probably I should tell her because she's smart and maybe has some money ideas like that sign thing. But she's also got stupid Charlotte Finley making her feel bad so I'm not gonna make it worse.

"Xbox," I say.

Now Bianca is putting back on all the covers I took off. "You said you were getting me a present."

"Yeah it's an airplane ticket to NASA so they can see if your brain has alien parts in it."

She falls asleep pretty soon. I stay up for a while and think about all the money I don't have and still need to get.

21

THE CONFESSION

JO

"SOUNDS like a cramp," Esther says.

She sits on my bed and reads an article on her phone. After Mass, I finally texted her to tell her what happened. Her mom drove her over right away.

"Or a twitch," she says.

I move my magnifying glass over the spot where Ronny's face hit on Friday night. If there was a crack, I would have found it by now—and I looked most of yesterday and today.

I say, "It felt like my muscles were frozen."

"Spontaneous, involuntary muscle contraction." Esther shows me the webpage. "That's what you had."

"A cramp."

"Yup. But you got through *Arioso*—"

"Oh no." I squint at a thin black line on the facing. Is that a crack? I press the facing, and the line moves. I inhale *fast* through my nose.

Esther joins me on the floor to look for herself. She touches the spot gently and lifts up a long black hair. "I believe this belongs to you."

I let out a long exhale. "I can't believe it didn't crack."

"I can't believe Ronny didn't get a concussion."

I say, "He told the nurses it would be hard to tell, because normally he exhibits concussed behavior."

Esther snorts. I hear the front door open and Ronny comes back to my room for the tenth time this weekend. He's dressed for a storm—a big winter jacket, snow pants, and boots. While I've been looking for cracks, he's been pushing his cart around the Apartments.

"Are you sure it's okay?" he asks.

"No cracks," I say. "How's your face?"

"Yeah fine." A purple circle covers most of his left cheek. "Like you're a hundred percent sure the cello is good."

"I can't find a crack."

"It looks like you got *punched*," Esther says.

"Yeah Jo's cello is bullying me and we're gonna tell the teachers Monday," he says.

"Any customers?" I ask.

"Actually yeah a lot of people go shopping on Sunday so I made like thirty bucks." Ronny swings his arms in circles. "But that wheel is busted bad so I gotta drag it by the front and pretty much my arms are killing me."

"Can you fix it?"

"I don't know it seems pretty broken. Like I was looking for a new one but it's just those Dollar Store ones and they're too small plus it's stealing so I just gotta use this one."

"Why don't you ask Mason?" Esther says. She stabs at her

phone with her thumbs. "Remember when he fixed the hinge on Jo's cello case? *Oh*, and the zipper on my book bag."

"You should ask him," I tell Ronny.

"Yeah remember I don't have a phone," he says.

"I just texted him." Esther's phone buzzes, and she reads it. "He said he can come over to look at it right now."

"Great but I'm working now so probably not." Ronny puts his winter gloves back on and fixes his hat. "Okay got like an hour before it's dark so bye and good job not finding a crack."

I hear him say goodbye to Mami and Papi in the kitchen, and then he leaves.

"He must really love playing Xbox," Esther says. Her phone buzzes again. "Mason says Ronny can bring it over to his house too."

"Tell him he left," I say.

She sends the message. "They used to hang out *all* the time in elementary school. Now I'm texting between them?"

I didn't know Ronny before he moved to the Apartments. We went to the same elementary school, but always had different teachers. "They still hang out."

"This one time, in fifth grade, they dressed up as a two-person horse for Halloween," Esther says. "It was so funny. They kept knocking over things in the classroom and fighting about who got to be the head or the butt. Our teacher made them take it off."

I laugh. "I remember that costume—from the parade at school." Did Ronny even dress up this past year? Bianca was a bug, but I think Ronny just wore a sweatshirt when we went trick-or-treating.

Esther stretches out on my bed and yawns. "I have to tell you something. But you can't tell anyone."

"Okay."

"Promise."

I say, "Just tell me."

She squeezes her eyes shut. "I kind of, sort of, *maybe* hope . . . that you don't get into Maple Hill."

"Why?" I sit on the other end of my bed. "You'll be first chair."

She finally opens her eyes. "I want to quit cello," she whispers.

"*What?*"

Esther sits up. "You can't tell anyone."

I say, "You can't quit—you're really good."

She sighs. "That's what my parents are going to say. And my cello teacher. And Mr. Newsum when I tell him at the end of the year." Esther lies back down. "Jo, we kind of *are* the cello section for orchestra and string ensemble."

Now I get it. "If I stay, you won't feel bad about quitting."

"That was the plan."

I whack her foot. "I thought you were mad I got an audition."

"Please. You were made for that place." She looks up at my posters of Carlos Prieto and Yo-Yo Ma. "You know that feeling you get when you're playing a cello piece, and you think it's the best thing in the whole world?"

"Yes."

"I *don't*," Esther says. "I like cello, but I don't love it like you. I want to try another instrument."

"Violin?"

We both laugh.

"The drums," she says.

"*Drums?*"

Esther plays an imaginary set of drums in the air. "The same place that did our cello camp has a *drum* camp. My brother went last year, and I want to go this summer. He's been giving me some lessons. Oh Jo—it's so fun."

"Wow," I say. "The drums."

"I had this whole plan where I sell my cello and use it to pay for the camp and lessons," she explains. "But now that you're leaving, should I stay?"

"No," I say. "Mr. Newsum will understand—he loves all music. Plus, I didn't even get into Maple Hill yet. Things might not change at all."

"You are *getting in*." Esther kicks me with her foot. "Say it."

Mr. Newsum's question bounces around my head. *If I think the cello makes the most beautiful sound in the world, then why don't I want people to hear me play it?*

Because I'm scared—duh.

But deep down, I know that's not a good enough reason.

"I'm getting in," I say.

22

MASON SAVES ME WITH
HIS SISTER'S PINK RAZOR SCOOTER

RONNY

"SO whose job is it to maintain roads?" Ms. Q says. "The national or state government?"

We're all looking at her and waiting for the answer. No wait not Bri because she's drawing this picture of a cat punching a guy in the face and I'm pretty sure it's me. I told everybody about the cello accident but she's doing her own story I guess.

"Or both?" Ms. Q says. "Remember it could be both."

Lots more staring.

"Guys, remember: Mr. Carrow will ask you this exact question on the Constitution test after the break," she says.

"National," says Julius.

Ms. Q goes over to Bri and now she's switching programs real quick to hide the picture.

"State," I say.

"Both," Ms. Q says. "Look at your charts."

I'm looking at the chart and see it. "Ha oh right both."

"So I was kinda right," Julius says.

"Yes, you and Ronny were *both* right," Ms. Q says. "Which is why it's in the *both* column."

We go over the rest of the practice questions and now I'm taking an online quiz. I get a low grade and take it again and do way better. Ms. Q lets us play computer games when we're done but mostly I'm googling *how to fix shopping cart wheels*. All of the videos are blocked and this is really not good because my arms are so tired from dragging that stupid thing by the front. This is a big shopping week for Christmas so probably I'm gonna have to ask Mason to fix it.

But then he's waiting at my locker after art and asks me on the way to lunch.

"So the wheel's broken?" he says.

"Yeah like it's wobbly and you can't steer it. I have to drag it to not crash."

"Probably needs a new wheel."

"Yeah."

"What's the cart for?"

"I'm taking people's stuff from the bus stop to their apartments for money. Like their grocery bags because a lot of them go shopping and then take the bus back and it's heavy and cold out."

"That's a good idea," he says.

"Ha yeah."

We're going to lunch and I tell him about the milk and egg destruction. "Yeah so I had to pay them all the money

I made but I made thirty-five bucks back yesterday so it's going good."

"I can put on a new wheel."

"Oh nice."

"Where's it at?"

"At my house like behind the building. I put it in this big bush so nobody steals it."

"Bring it to my house after school," he says. "Or do you have that thing with Jo at the senior citizen place."

"Not on Mondays," I say. "Okay thanks."

Now we're in the cafeteria and I'm getting in line to buy lunch. Mason has his lunch in one of those cool boxes I used to bring before the school paid for my food. "What do you think about neon pink," he says.

"Like the color?"

"Yeah. The color on that girl's shirt," he says and he's pointing at this girl's shirt that says *Kennesaw Cheer* in neon-pink letters.

"I mean it's pretty bright," I say and I'm putting pizza on my tray. I get fries and corn too and some chocolate milk. Now we're at the register with the lunch lady so why is he still even here?

"That could be good," he says. "People will see you better."

"What?"

"Number," says the lunch lady and I say it real fast. She types it in and why is she looking at my tray weird? "Only one side hon," she says.

"Yeah I got fries."

"And corn."

"Come on corn is a vegetable," I say.

"Corn is a grain and a vegetable," Mason says. "Technically."

"Fine I'll put it back," I say and now I'm getting gross green beans instead. The lady rings me up and finally we're going to our lunch table. "Okay so I'll take the bus home and bring it over."

"Bring Cheez-Its," he says. "If you have any."

"Yeah my mom gets those little bag ones."

"Not Cheese Nips."

"Yeah they're Cheez-Its."

"Bring a couple. Maybe four."

"Okay," I say. "What are Cheese Nips?"

"Fake Cheez-Its," he says. "They're the worst."

Jo has string ensemble today so I'm riding the bus home by myself. I tell my dad I'm going to Mason's which is across the highway in a big development but it's like maybe twenty minutes if you're walking fast. I'll be dragging a cart so probably longer.

"*Mason*," he says. He's in the bathroom with all the cleaning spray bottles because he does all that stuff now if his back isn't hurting too bad. "How's he doing? Been a long time since you went over there."

"Yeah he's gonna help me fix the wheel on my cart."

"Gotcha. And then you're going 'to work'?"

"Yeah if he can do it fast."

"Okay. Be back before dark."

I grab a couple little Cheez-It bags and go get the cart. There's some flurries on it from the tiny snow last night so I'm brushing them off and now I'm dragging it down the sidewalk. It takes forever to get to the light where the bus stop is and now I'm going across the highway into Mason's giant neighborhood. It's got one of those big signs that says *Fairways Community* and a pair of golf clubs because there's a golf course in here and some people's backyards is the putting green.

Man, my arms are killing me and I keep having to stop for breaks and I'm super sweaty when I get there. His house is one of those bigger ones on a street with like twenty houses that look the same except for different Christmas stuff. Mason's dad likes the blow-up ones so probably he's got twenty in his front yard. They're all deflated now on the snowy ground but at night it looks cool.

"Hey," he says when I go in the little side garage door.

"Hey."

"Where's the cart?"

"Outside."

He opens the garage door and now we're pulling it in. There's a bunch of tools on the ground and a pink Razor Scooter.

"Which is the bad wheel?" Mason says.

We flip the cart upside down and now I'm showing him. "Pretty wobbly."

"It's really worn down."

"Yeah."

He's looking at the bent side part where I kicked it a ton. "What happened?"

"Yeah that was when I crashed," I say. "With those ladies I was telling you about."

Mason starts unscrewing stuff. He's got the bad wheel off pretty quick and now he's unscrewing one of the pink wheels from the scooter.

"So you don't ride that anymore?" I say.

"It's not mine."

"Ha what?"

The inside door opens and his older sister Julia is coming out with big headphones and a phone. *"He's in the garage with Ronny!"* she's saying back into the house.

Mason gets the Razor Scooter wheel off and measures it on the cart. "Fits pretty good."

"What are you doing?" Julia comes over and now she's taking off her headphones. "That's mine."

"You don't ride it," Mason says.

"Seriously, stop."

"Did you bring the other thing?" he says.

I get the Cheez-It bags out and he's giving them all to Julia. She looks at them and is opening one. Probably she eats for like a minute just standing there watching him put her pink Razor Scooter wheel onto my cart.

"Our mom only buys Cheese Nips," Mason says.

Julia is making happy eating sounds. "It's not even the same snack."

"I didn't know there was even another one," I say.

Mason tightens all the screws and now we're turning the cart back over. I push it back and forth and wow it's way easier.

"Oh man that's awesome," I say.

"Let's test it outside."

He pushes it across the driveway a little and lets go. Instead of going to the left it now goes to the right pretty hard.

"It's higher than the other wheel," he says.

"Yeah but it's better than dragging it."

"You'll crash again and have to pay people for the stuff you broke."

"Yeah maybe."

We take it back in the garage and he's taking off the other Razor Scooter wheel. "They have to be even. And you need a parking brake so if you stop on a hill it won't roll away."

"Yeah okay."

"Hey," Julia says and how many bags has she eaten? "What if I want to ride that?"

"You got this last Christmas and never used it," Mason says.

"Maybe I want to."

"You're getting a hoverboard this year."

Some Cheez-It crumbs are stuck on her lips. "I am?"

He's pointing at the work bench. "By the paint."

Julia goes over and is looking under a bunch of tarps. "Oh. My. *Gosh*." She's going back inside now and texting like crazy on her phone.

"Ha maybe next year we can make it a hover cart," I say.

Mason gets the second wheel on and we're taking it for another test ride. It's even faster and goes totally straight when you let go. Now he's using some big pliers to fix the side I kicked in so it's not as bent and then he adds this lock thing made from a piece of metal onto the back wheel. When I press it down with my foot, it keeps the wheel from moving, but when I lift it things roll like normal.

"Bianca says I should have a sign so people know I want their money," I say.

"That's a good idea. You should put your name and price on it."

"Yeah like 'Ronny's Grocery Delivery: I will probably not crash and break your food.'"

He's digging around in a box of wood by the workbench and finds a square piece. Now he's giving me a big Sharpie and we keep saying a bunch of ideas until we get the best one for the sign and I write:

Ronny's Delivery Service
I haul food and stuff
$10 a load
or $5 if you
can't pay $10
Thanks

Mason gets his dad's drill and he's putting holes in each corner and uses pink zip ties to connect it to the one side. "So they match the wheels."

We put a bunch of heavy stuff inside to see how much it

can take and zoom around the driveway. Mason tightens a couple things on each wheel and then wraps some cool grip tape around the handle so it's not as slippery. Now he's putting on some old Christmas lights that use batteries so people can see me coming.

"I mean this is pretty cool," I say. "Like probably this is the best shopping cart ever."

"Yeah it's pretty cool."

Probably I have like half an hour before it gets dark. "Okay I'm gonna go see if I can deliver some stuff on my way home."

"Are you and Jo going out?" he says.

"Jo Ramos?"

"Yeah."

"Come on hahahaha." I can see my breath in big giant clouds as I laugh. "Jo Ramos?"

"You hang out every day."

"Yeah we're doing that thing at the Manor."

"You hang out every day anyway."

"Okay," I say and is he serious? "I mean I live twenty feet from her so yeah we hang out a lot."

"You're not that far from my house. My mom could drive me like before. I could bring my Xbox."

"Yeah," I say. I'm looking way up on the garage shelf at something and is that the horse costume from fifth grade? Haha man that was funny but also so sweaty and hot. "I mean my house is pretty small and Bianca is always being annoying so probably not."

"We can hang out here," he says. "Julia thinks the basement smells, so the TV is ours."

Julia comes out again. "Mom wants to know if Ronny is staying for dinner."

It's real quiet for a second and now Mason is saying, "Ronny has to go to work."

"But Ronny is coming back for dinner another time," I say and Mason is nodding and smiling. "Probably soon and there will be lots of Xboxing so get ready."

"You got weirder," Julia says to me but who cares because now I'm zooming down the sidewalk back toward the highway. The wheels are so fast and so straight that I can ride it basically the whole way home just pushing with my one foot and standing on the bottom rack.

23

THE PRIVATE CONCERT

JO

I finish my song and get a drink from the practice room sink. Mr. Newsum emailed me some wrist exercises after I told him what happened on Friday, so I do those too.

"Sounds lovely," Nurse Monica tells me when I leave through the office. "I could listen to it all day."

In the cafe, I grab a rice pudding and go sit with Ronny at a table with two other residents. One has short, curly white hair and glasses with thick frames—Jeanie, I think. Her friend Jean has a brown wig and hearing aids that don't seem to fit right.

"Jo, nobody here has ever had a peanut butter and Fluff sandwich," Ronny tells me. "Like can you believe that?"

I say, "It does have a lot of sugar."

"Ha right."

"Do they put the marshmallows into the peanut butter jar?" Jeanie asks.

"No, the Fluff is in its own jar," Ronny explains. "Probably it's like a hundred marshmallows melted down into liquid and that's one jar. You put it on the bread like jelly but it's marshmallow so together it's peanut butter and Fluff."

"I like apple butter," Jean says loudly. "Easier on the stomach."

"I don't think that's a thing," Ronny says. "Probably you mean apple sauce."

"Apple *butter*," Jean says even louder.

"You're shouting," says Jeanie. She reaches over and pats my hand. "Josefina: How is your wrist feeling?"

"Better," I say. "Thanks for asking."

"Better than Ronald's face," Jean says. She and Jeanie laugh with their eyes shut.

"Hey I'm a hero," Ronny says. "Probably they're gonna be telling that story around here for a hundred years."

"We can barely remember our names some days," says Jeanie. "How are we going to remember yours?"

"Where am I?" Jean shouts. "This isn't my house." She pretends to be scared, and then giggles with Jeanie. "And who's this young man at my table making up stories about jars of liquid marshmallows."

"*Hahaha*," Ronny says. I laugh so hard, my ribs hurt.

Ms. Sarah walks over to our table. "Ladies, Ronny: Sorry to break up the party, but can I steal our cellist?"

"There are no seats open at *this* table," Noreen calls over to us. She points at Ronny. "Am I understood?"

"Yes, thank you, Noreen," Ms. Sarah says.

"I mean I'm no Richard but I been pretty nice to her," Ronny tells Ms. Sarah.

"You've been more than nice. Keep it up."

I get my cello and follow Ms. Sarah to a room on the other side of the Manor. We walk into a small entryway that has a bathroom and two doors with name tags. The door on the right says *Eleanor* and the one on the left says *Harold*. A nurse goes into Harold's room with a tray of food and closes the door behind her.

"Not all residents make the journey to the cafe," Ms. Sarah says. "Some are too sick. Some don't want to go."

"Why not?"

She tucks her clipboard under one arm and thinks. "Who do you sit with at lunch?"

"My friends."

"But what if they weren't there? Maybe it would be easier to eat in the library. Better than sitting alone."

"Yes. Maybe it would."

She points to the ceiling. "No intercoms in the rooms, so I thought we could bring the concert to them."

I look around the small space. The sound will be good—and private. "I like that idea."

"Music therapy is apparently doing wonders these days. I just read the most fascinating study on mood and pain management. Even faster recovery times."

I say, "That makes sense. The best I ever feel is when I'm playing."

Ms. Sarah goes inside each room and talks quietly with the residents. I get a chair from the hallway and trim off some bow hairs. She comes back out but leaves each of the doors open a few inches.

"Okay, we're ready." She checks her watch. "I'll be back in ten, and then you're off the clock."

I turn my chair and look at both doors. I think about Harold and Eleanor, stuck in their rooms. A song to cheer them up . . .

I jump right into Popper's Etude #1, the technical practice piece I'll play at my audition. It sounds like two horses racing across a field—a full-speed gallop over rocks, ditches, and creeks. My fingers jump from string to string with them, trying to keep up with the bowing. They slow to zig and zag around boulders, and then it sounds like they might fall or get tired—but then they take off again.

I play faster the second time. I think about Harold moving his head back and forth—Eleanor tapping her fingers on the bed. No one can stay still during Popper. The third time, I fly through the notes and finish covered in sweat. I drag the sweatband across my forehead, and play it one more time— slow and dramatic. When it's over, I take deep breaths and stretch my wrist out. I hear a small clap from inside one of the rooms, but I can't tell which one.

"Thank you," I say. In the quiet, I realize something else.

I'm not nervous.

The bees aren't just asleep—the hive is gone. Instead, a wave of warm sunshine rushes from the bottom of my toes to the top of my head and back down. I feel incredible.

It wasn't Bach, and it wasn't perfect, but it made sense—like it was the exact right thing to do with the cello in these ten minutes.

Better than nailing an audition at Maple Hill.

Ten auditions, actually.

"Just wait till you see it," Ronny tells me the whole bus ride and walk home. "Like it's going to blow your mind."

At our apartment building, he disappears around the back. A minute later, he returns with the upgraded shopping cart.

I say, "Wow. This looks much better."

"I know right? Yeah and Mason gave me an old bike lock so I can like hook it to the bush so nobody steals it."

"Good idea."

He points at the sign. "Check out the sign."

"Nice."

"Hey put your cello in, I'll show you how good it is."

I say, "Maybe my backpack instead."

"Haha yeah good idea."

The cart flies down the sidewalk to the parking lot. Ronny shows me how easy it is to steer now, and how he can push off with one foot while riding on the bottom bracket. He rides in circles around me, and then lets me try.

"Christmas is ten days away so people will be shopping like crazy this weekend," he says. "I'll be out the whole time freezing my butt off, but oh man I'm gonna make so much money."

"Why are the wheels pink?"

"Ha long story," he says.

We sit on the playground swings and he tells me how Mason fixed the cart. The sun goes down and Christmas lights twinkle all over the Apartments. My toes are frozen, but I don't want to go inside.

I say, "I wish I had another two hundred dollars to give you."

Ronny blows out long clouds of misty air above his head. "I mean you could sell your cello and ha that would buy like three cars."

"I'm serious."

"But no good because then you couldn't get into cello school with all the uniforms and good lunches." He pumps his legs and swings higher. He won't look at me. "I mean I'll have three cars but you'll have to keep going to our school and eat orange pizza and never be a cello master."

"Are you mad I'm leaving?"

"Haha what?"

"It's not funny," I say—almost shout. "I don't even know if I really want to go."

"*Okay fine so don't go,*" he yells back. "And yeah it's actually funny." He leaps off the swing and lands on the frozen ground. He points to the townhomes behind the Apartments. "Probably it's the most hilarious thing ever in all of history because I got Charlotte Finley up there painting over unicorns and saying dumb stuff to Bianca, plus whoever the crap lives in my room playing Xbox on his giant TV and I'm down here in FINAL NOTICE land with canceled Christmas and you're leaving for cello school okay. Probably it's the funniest thing ever in the whole stupid universe so HAHA FREAKING HA!"

A woman looks out her curtain in a nearby apartment window.

Ronny walks to the basketball court and picks up a deflated ball. He runs into the open field toward the townhomes and throws it as hard as he can. It doesn't go that far.

I run after him, and we stare up at his old house. The new people decorated the deck with pretty lights that blink every few seconds.

I say, "My room window faces that way too."

He wipes his nose. "It was a pretty good house."

"Why are they so tall?"

"I don't know, they have a lot of stairs."

I grab him by the shoulders and make him face me. "I'm glad you live here now. And if I get into Maple Hill, you'll be the person I miss the most." My voice wobbles. "Okay?"

He nods. Water fills the pockets under his eyes. "Me too."

I hug him.

After a few seconds, he lets go. "Probably this is why people think we're going out."

"Gross," I say.

"Haha."

Ronny puts the basketball back on the court. We count Santas on our way home and guess how many inches it will snow.

24

VINCE IS AN ICE CREAM EATING MONSTER

RONNY

"MAYBE we'll get out early tomorrow," I say.

Ms. Q is shaking her head. "It's not going to start snowing until after school. Three o'clock, I think."

I look out the windows in her room and see zero snow. But there's clouds and it's all gray and really cold so you can feel it coming. "Yeah but maybe it will start early."

"They never let us out early," Bri says.

"We had four days off last February, remember?" Ms. Q says. "It snowed over two feet."

"Yeah that was awesome," I say.

Ms. Q is checking the review answer key on Bri's computer. "I didn't love going the extra days in the summer," Ms. Q says.

"Yeah that was bad but it's so good when you have the snow day," I say. "Like you know it's gonna be bad later but probably you wouldn't change it for anything because it's so good now."

"Taylor Swift knows when it's going to snow," Bri says.

"Ha really?"

"She gets in my lap and shivers all day before it snows."

"Come on," I say. "Your cat sings and knows the weather, no way."

"Maybe she can sense the temperature change," Ms. Q says. "She *is* an animal."

"What did she do this morning?" I say.

Bri is smiling real big. "She was shaking all during breakfast."

"Oh man," I say. "Probably that means a blizzard."

I keep looking out the window and thinking I see flurries all period. Snow is gonna be good for business because I'll be off school and when the roads are clear I can zoom around the whole day.

"You should shovel snow," Mason says at lunch. "Do you have a shovel?"

"Yeah."

"My neighbors pay me twenty to shovel their whole driveway."

"Whoa really?"

"Yeah."

"But we don't have driveways," I say. "Like at the Apartments it's just sidewalks and stuff and guys with snowblowers come and do it the next night."

"So do it first," Mason says. "And you could clean off people's cars too."

"My dad *hates* doing that," Esther says. "Our garage is full of stuff, so he always has to park outside, and it always gets covered in snow."

"Oh man," I say and my brain is spinning real fast. "This is gonna be amazing."

"What if you made flyers and handed them out today?" Jo says. "That way our neighbors know you're available to do it."

"Yeah and put my prices on it."

Mason is getting his laptop out and now he's clicking around. "I'll put your email on it too so they can tell you if they want it done."

"Guys, wait," I say and oh man my brain is smashing great ideas together. "We should put my cart business on there. Like maybe tell them about that too if they need it this weekend or next week."

Mason types like crazy and Esther reads it off his screen. "*Ronny's Home Services. Now offering: Carting your stuff from bus stop to your door, sidewalk snow shoveling, cleaning snow off your car.*"

"Okay but how much?" I say. "That's a lot of different stuff."

Mason is typing some more and Esther is making a weird face. "*Pay me whatever you think it's worth?*" she says.

"Come on, what if it's a dollar," I say. "Like I shovel your walkway and you only pay me a dollar?"

"I don't think someone would pay you just a dollar," Jo says. "Loretta paid you five dollars, and you didn't even ask her for any money."

"Yeah but she's really nice. Probably most people aren't like that."

Mason is lifting his computer up to my face. "Smile."

"What?"

He hits a button and then does more clicking. Esther is nodding and then Mason turns the computer so we can all see my face. I'm smiling like *huh what?* and you can see some kids in the background.

"It's good," he says. "It's funny."

"Come on I look weird."

"That's your normal face," Esther says. She's looking at Jo now. "Right? That's his normal face."

Jo is laughing and nodding. "Usually."

"Oh man wow."

Mason puts my face on top of a clip-art house and at the bottom he types *Service is my goal. My goal is service.* "I saw it on a commercial."

"Guys this is amazing," I say and now I'm making the same face on the flyer. "Probably everyone will want to hire this face like who wouldn't?"

I get off the bus and run real fast to my apartment. I tell my dad I'll be at the bus stop so Bianca can come find me and now I'm going back outside to get the cart. Pretty soon I'm shoving the flyers in the door cracks and under people's mats so they know about all my services. I do the building next to us and across from us and the one next to that but probably I need to save a couple in case people coming off the bus want some.

"Hey there, young man," a lady says and it's Loretta waving at me from her door.

"Hey," I say. "It's gonna snow like crazy tomorrow and that's coming from a pretty smart cat."

"That's what I hear. Got the aching bones to prove it." She's reading the flyer real close to her face. "My son used to come by and shovel for me, but he works in the city now."

"Oh yeah, I can do it."

"Put me down for a sidewalk clearing."

"Come on you don't have to pay me."

"Honest work deserves an honest wage."

"Yeah but my mom said I have to help old people for free," I say. "I mean senior citizens."

Her face becomes all wrinkles and she laughs real hard. "Maybe I'll pay you with some cookies. Homemade this time."

"Yeah but how will I know because you lied before?" I say and we're both laughing now.

I zoom down to the bus stop and see some people are carrying stuff but nothing too heavy.

"You joking," somebody says.

I look over and it's the tall and short ladies whose stuff I ruined with the milk explosion.

"Hey," I say.

They're coming and checking my cart out. Their puffy coats aren't zipped and I can see name tags on their red Target work shirts. *Samantha* is the short one and the tall one who got really angry is *Symphony*.

"Whoa cool name," I say. "My friend wants to play in a symphony one day for musical geniuses."

She's pretty much staring but now kind of smiling at me. "And you're Ronny."

"Present."

"Nice lights," says Samantha.

"Yeah and new wheels with a brake so no more crashing."

"Where'd you get all this?"

"My friend Mason built it for me."

"That's a good friend."

"Yeah probably he can build anything." I'm giving them one of the extra flyers I didn't get rid of. "I'm doing snow shoveling too if you need that done."

"I like to shovel," Symphony says. She has these really skinny eyebrows and they're all pointed down now looking at me. "What about laundry?"

"Ha I don't do laundry."

They're both laughing. "Would you carry it to the laundromat is what I'm asking." Symphony is pointing to the shops on the other side of the parking lot.

"Oh yeah I mean sure."

"Kid gonna be a millionaire," Samantha says.

I follow them to the way back apartment buildings and

they're putting these big giant bags in the cart. It's heavy but Mason fixed it so good pushing is super easy and I'm barely working that hard at all. Like now I have to slow down for them to keep up and when we get to the laundromat I'm not even that tired. I push the cart inside and now I'm putting their bags on the washing machines.

"Yeah sorry again about the eggs and milk," I say. "Probably I should do this one for free."

"Hold on, hold on," Samantha says. She makes a face at Symphony, who does some eye rolling and now is digging out some money from her purse.

"Not all the eggs were broken," Symphony says and gives me a five. "And you did good work."

"Whoa thanks. I'd take it back for you but I can't work after dark."

"We can handle it. Do it every week." Symphony starts putting stuff in the washer. She stops for a second and she's smiling for real this time so I can see all her teeth. "Merry Christmas, Ronny."

"Yeah Merry Christmas."

I go outside and I'm putting the money in my wallet. It's not a ton but it's five dollars closer oh man it feels amazing to have this cart and a snow service and maybe some days off. And it's not even four so I got more time before it gets dark plus all the snow coming this weekend and the Christmas shopping.

"Nice cart."

I look over and there's this big guy with a big giant beard standing outside the Dairy Queen. He's got the biggest size Blizzard but it looks tiny in his huge hands. Pretty sure I've seen him before.

"Ha thanks," I say but who eats ice cream when it's freezing out?

"They used to close this place in the winter," he says and now he's pointing at the Dairy Queen. "I'm glad they don't anymore."

He goes over to a giant red tow truck with a metal cross thing sticking up in the back and now I'm reading these gold letters on the side that say *Vince's Towing*.

25

CHRISTMAS CAROLS

JO

"I mean who eats Dairy Queen in the winter?" Ronny asks me. "Like come on, right before a giant storm. He probably puts weird candy in it like Nerds."

I wave goodbye to Mami as she drives out of the Manor's parking lot. A ceiling of clouds covers the sky. I can almost feel the snow about to fall. "I thought Dairy Queen closed in the winter."

"Yeah well they don't and Vince from Vince's Towing is loving it."

We sign in at the front desk, and then get a snack in the cafe.

"He's like the Grinch," Ronny says. "Like he has no heart or maybe his heart is frozen and ice cream isn't even cold to him. Probably it's warm like the sun."

I say, "Maybe he just likes ice cream."

"Come on what kind of person takes people's cars for a job? Pretty much his job is stealing stuff and messing up people's lives."

"Tow trucks help people too," I say. "I see them on the way to my aunt's. Cars have problems on the highway and the tow trucks pull them away."

Ronny jams his cup against the drink machine. A stream of juice flies out. "If Vince the car stealer had a broken back and needed me to cart around his Christmas family dinner I'd zoom the opposite way at like a hundred miles an hour."

"You would not."

"Yeah I would because he'd steal our car in the dark when we're sleeping and not care at all. Probably he'd go to Dairy Queen after."

"Ronny." I point to the cafe window—snowflakes.

"Oh man," he says. "Here it comes."

Mami texts me about the snow. I find Ms. Sarah and I tell her that my mom will have to pick us up early if the snow gets worse. She says that's fine, and I go to my practice room. I run through all my exercises—breathing, wrist, scales, and études. Over the intercom, I play my full audition set of songs that I will perform at the Friday concert tonight—*Arioso*, and the D Minor and G Major preludes. A few mistakes, but nothing to worry about. If that had been in front of the Maple Hill string faculty, I'd feel good about my chances of being accepted. OPERATION FINAL NOTICE: PHASE JO would have been a success, and my next cello adventure could begin. That's what I want, right?

So shouldn't I be more excited about it?

I think about Harold and Eleanor—that warm wave of

sunshine I felt during their private concert. I grab my cello and walk down to their rooms. Both doors are shut, so I ask a nurse walking by if they are okay.

"Oh, they're fine," she says. "Just sleeping."

I see the hallway clock. 3:32 p.m. Ninety minutes until the concert. A few bees wake up.

"I am nervous," I say to the empty hallway. "It's normal to be nervous before a performance."

I don't want to go back to the practice room yet, so I walk to the end of the hallway. I find a small room with soft leather chairs and a couch. They face two glass doors that lead to a courtyard with a fountain in the middle. Christmas lights cover the bushes. Big, fluffy snowflakes pile up on the stone walkway. Ronny should be able to make a lot of money shoveling tomorrow.

Behind me, I hear a chirp. I look over and see a large cage with tiny black birds. They flap and dive the closer I get.

"Finches," Ms. Sarah says behind me. "They're supposed to be calming."

"It is very peaceful in here."

"We call it the Serenity Room." She points out the doors. "In the summer, residents come to watch the fountain in the sun. In the winter, the lights and the snow. Sometimes I come here when I'm having a bad day. The finches and the view have a nice recharging effect."

A resident walks around the corner very slowly. Her skin is darker like mine, and she's wearing a Rudolph the

Red-Nosed Reindeer sweater that has a red light on his nose.

"Rose, you look lovely," Ms. Sarah says. "A bit far from home, though."

Rose sits down very carefully in one of the soft leather chairs. "We wanted to watch the snow."

"We?"

Another resident comes around the corner, and then three more.

"Hello, dear," one says to me. She's small—almost my size. Her eyes are wide with excitement. "Would you play us something? I think that would make this an absolutely perfect afternoon."

I take a quick breath in through my nose. "Okay."

Ms. Sarah brings me a chair, and I set up near the door so I don't block the view of the courtyard. "Good luck," she says.

What should I play? Something peaceful, but not sad. A song that sounds like falling snow on a courtyard fountain. Do I know a song like that? I do another fast inhale.

"Do you know 'Winter Wonderland'?" Rose asks.

"Oh, I love that song," says one of the other residents. "One of my favorites."

"It's perfect," says the woman with wide eyes. "Do you know it?"

"Yes," I say—of course I do. I just wasn't expecting to play Christmas carols.

Have I ever even *played* Christmas carols? I don't think so. Usually all my practice time goes to difficult sections of a piece I'm learning, or an exercise that will help me with that difficult section.

I don't think I've even taken a request—ever.

"I've never played it, though," I say. "But I could try."

"Oh, just follow us," Rose says. "Give us a note."

I give her a high C. She tries it out, but doesn't like it.

"Something lower?" she asks.

I give her a G.

Suddenly, they're all singing.

They forget the words a few times, correct each other, then lose the beat and find it again. At the end of the first verse I join them. It's not a hard song to play, and I make some mistakes, but none of them notice. I sing too, because we're singing "Winter Wonderland" while looking out onto an actual winter wonderland.

When the song ends, Rose points to her blinking sweater and starts right up with "Rudolph the Red-Nosed Reindeer." I lead with the melody this time, shouting the funny lines like *like a lightbulb* between lyrics. Out of nowhere, a deep bass voice joins in behind me—Carl, holding one arm out like an opera singer. The ladies clap and shriek and we sing it all over again. They beg Carl to do a solo.

"If you insist." He clears his throat. "Josefina: An A, if you could."

Carl booms a dramatic version of "O Holy Night" in perfect pitch. He waves me in, so I play the deeper harmony to make his melody stand out. We sing it twice, and then he nods for me to keep going. I play the melody alone, using only the notes in my head. I hit two sharp and one *way* flat. I wince at the mistake, but no one else does—their eyes are closed. They sway their heads back and forth to my solo, smiles across their faces. I am warm from head to toe.

"Bravo!" Carl shouts when I finish. He bows low. "Now, I must go change. Josefina, I shall see you soon."

I say, "You look fine."

"This?" He frowns and shakes his head. "I'm about to attend a concert with the famous *Josefina*—I need to look my best. Ta-ta."

The rest of us watch the snow. Rose tells a story about a blizzard from when she was a little girl—snowdrifts six feet high. It seems like only a few minutes have gone by when Ms. Sarah taps me on the shoulder.

"Showtime," she says.

26

RONNY VS. RICHARD

RONNY

I'M staring out the cafe window at the snow. Oh man this is gonna be amazing it's already like an inch. Now I'm getting my sixth cup of juice and going back to sit with Jean and Jeanie.

"It's pretty much a blizzard," I say.

"I *love* a good snow," Jeanie says. "So pretty."

"But think of the accidents," Jean says. "Roads will be a mess."

"What do you care? You're not driving."

"Those plows take up the whole road," Jean says. "And then there's the shoveling."

Jeanie is shaking her head. "What do you have to shovel?"

"I'm gonna shovel a ton," I say and now I'm looking over at Noreen's table in the way back. Some guy is there with her in a black suit and is he my dad's age? He's got a briefcase and his tie is all loose and mostly he's been looking at his phone the whole time.

"Who's that guy with Noreen?" I say.

They look over and now they're making faces at each other.

"That's Richard," Jeanie tells me. "Noreen's son."

"Oh man, *Richard*? I didn't know he was real."

"He never comes by," Jean says and she's rolling her eyes. "He's a *lawyer*. They're very *busy*."

The kitchen people start cleaning up and there's Jo going into the Lounge. I take Jean's and Jeanie's plates to the counter and then Noreen is rolling by me in her wheelchair.

"That's him," she says to Richard. "The child who tried to kill me. Before that, he tried to burn my mouth."

"Yeah not really," I say. "I tripped and the other thing was more like a reheating situation."

"I'm gonna say this once," Richard says in this real mean voice but then he smiles and is waving at me? Oh, he's got in one of those ear things where you can talk on the phone. "If that report isn't in my inbox tonight, you can forget about that contract going in the mail."

Jean and Jeanie are shaking their heads at him.

I go to the bathroom because of all the juice and now I'm at the front door to see the snow. Oh man it's up to my ankles already and coming down faster and faster which is really good for business. Jo is on the sidewalk doing her thirty-second freezing cold thing to stop sweating so I go out there too.

"Okay, so are you ready?" I say. "You're gonna do awesome."

Jo is looking really happy and is she even freaking out? "I feel good."

"Whoa so no bees?"

"I don't know." She's smiling and oh man she's never looked this happy before playing. "I just feel *good*."

"Haha," I say and throw snow on her because this is an OPERATION FINAL NOTICE Christmas miracle.

We go back in and I'm getting a seat with Jean and Jeanie in the second row. Noreen is in the front with Richard and is he still on his phone? Now Carl is coming over and sitting with us in this super-fancy suit and tie.

"Well look at *you*," Jeanie says. "Do you need a date?"

Jean slaps her arm. "He's already got one. Me."

"Ladies, ladies, I can escort you both." He's bowing to Jean and Jeanie and now he's trying to make his tie tighter but his fingers are all shaky. I've seen my mom do this for my dad when he wore a tie for Christmas church so now I'm helping make the knot smaller on Carl's tie. "Thank you, young man."

"You look pretty awesome," I say.

He's winking and giving everybody around us these sugar-free Tic Tacs. "Have you seen the snow?"

"Yeah I was just out there it's crazy."

"I just hope the power doesn't go out again," Jean says. "What a nightmare that was during the storm last year."

"Ha what?" I say but Sarah is up in the front telling everybody to be quiet.

"And here we are again, friends," she says. "Our third concert this month, and we are again very privileged to have

Josefina Ramos. As you know by now, she is incredibly talented, and we are so blessed to have her play several times a week over the PA. But there is nothing like a live sound, especially with her instrument, so we're glad she's back—and it's snowing! Could it be more perfect? Okay: Let's give Jo a warm Manor welcome once again."

They clap and Jo is already all set up but isn't playing yet. She's just sitting there and smiling and now she's standing up?

"Thank you for letting me come here and play," she says. "It's one of the best parts of my day."

I think she's gonna say more but she sits down and whips her braid back. She's closing her eyes and breathing real slow in and out, in and out. She's not freaking out at all like you can see it on her face. She's in the zone but what was with that speech? Now she's got her arm up and ready to play in front of maybe forty people and she's like a real performer or something.

Oh man she's turning into Carlos Prieto.

It's real quiet except for Noreen's oxygen thing going *cushhhh cushhh cushhh*. Jo does her counting-in thing and moves her head down like she's about to start when Richard's phone rings.

"Sorry," he says and he's putting in the ear thing and talking already. We're all watching him go outside the big front doors and talk real loud like he's the president of America or something. Noreen looks around and can't find him and, man, is she scared? Her eyes are real wide and she keeps reaching her hand out where Richard was sitting.

Cushhh cushh cushhh goes her machine and Jo is lifting her bow. Now she's doing her counting thing again.

And now the whole room goes dark.

"Oh great," Jean says.

It stays real quiet for a couple seconds and there's a really long *beeeeeeeeeeeeeeeeeeeeep* and now Sarah is shouting *everybody stay calm everyone stay calm, the generators will turn on momentarily* but people aren't staying calm like at all. I mean you'd think old people couldn't be that loud but like they're all talking and the nurses are yelling and oh man somebody is screaming?

And now somebody is banging really loud like way behind us. I look back and it's Richard banging on the door like crazy because he's freezing his butt off outside. But that screaming is getting worse and it sounds like Bri's cat doing her worst singing ever and it's getting louder and louder.

The *beeeeeeeeeeeeeep* sound stops and some yellow ceiling lights turn on. It's still pretty dark but you can see a little and now I see the screaming is coming from *Noreen.* Maybe she's crying who knows but the nurses are all zooming around past her so I quick go over.

"Hey hey hey it's okay," I say. "It's just snow we're gonna be okay."

"I think something's wrong with her," Jo says. "She needs help."

I'm looking around and there's Nurse Monica waving this little flashlight. "Hey something is wrong here can you help?" I say.

Somebody grabs my hand real hard and is crushing my bones. Like it really hurts and I look down and it's Noreen and she's got these big wide scared eyes. "Richard," she says in this whiney scream. *"Richard."*

"It's Ronny, but you're okay," I say. "They're gonna fix it right?"

"Noreen—look at me, Noreen," Monica says. She's checking her oxygen tank and tubes and now she's feeling her pulse. "You're gonna be fine. Everything is fine. I need you to breathe easy. The power will be back on soon."

Oh man Noreen's grip is like a robot clamp thing and I fix my hand so she's not breaking my knuckles. "Is she okay?" I say.

"She's fine," Monica says. "Just stay with her and help her keep calm. We need to go check on the residents who are in their rooms."

"Yeah okay."

"Ohhhhhh," Noreen whines and she's leaning her head on my shoulder and grabbing my arm with her other hand. *"Oh noooo."*

"It's okay it's really gonna be fine," I say and squeeze her hands really hard even though pretty much I can't feel mine anymore. "At my old house we always lost power but it comes back on trust me."

She's shutting her eyes really tight and I see some tears coming out. She's shaking so bad it's making me shake and I keep squeezing her hand harder and I think maybe that's helping. Richard is still banging on the door like a big giant idiot and now he's yelling *hey hey hey* and where the crap did Jo go?

Daaaaaaaaadadadadadadadd.

Cello is coming through the PA system really loud. It's like Jo turned the volume on the speaker all the way up and it's not a fancy song like she usually plays but—

"Hahaha," I laugh and now I'm singing with the words real loud. "*You would even say it glows—like a lightbulb. Then all the other reindeer, used to laugh and call him names—like Pinocchio—*"

She just keeps playing it over and over again and more and more people are singing. Wow Carl is really getting into it with a professional voice and now the whole room is going at it. Noreen isn't crying anymore or shaking but she's still holding on to me pretty tight. She's saying something so I lean closer to hear it.

". . . *Rudolph with your nose so bright, won't you guide my sleigh tonight . . .*"

I sing with her for a couple seconds and then the lights come on like the sun is blasting us. Man, it's so bright and Noreen is crying again a little but mainly from being happy I think.

"See I knew it," I say. "It always comes back on. I mean that was pretty fast actually."

"Mom," Richard says and he's coming back inside with snow all over him. Now he's kneeling down on the other side of Noreen and patting her leg. "Mom, I'm sorry—I got locked out."

Noreen won't look at him and keeps holding on to me. I actually have to pee really bad and try to get up but she won't let go. Jo keeps playing and the nurses run back and forth and then Sarah finally comes back and is that Jo's dad with her?

"That was certainly *not* on the agenda," Sarah says to everybody. "But much better than when we lost power last year."

Noreen shakes a ton when Sarah says *last year* and is Richard even helping?

"The new backup generators did their job, so we can all relax," Sarah says. "Unfortunately, our cellist needs to get home before the roads become more dangerous, so we'll have to wait until our Christmas party next Wednesday to hear her performance."

There's a lot of *ohhhs* and *nooooos* but then Carl is standing up and clapping and now everybody is clapping. Jo comes out and talks to her dad and they're waving at me but oh man I can't get Noreen to let go.

"I gotta go," I say. "Remember I don't live here and it's snowing really bad. I mean I'll be back on Tuesday but I really gotta go."

She's nodding up and down real hard. "You'll come back."

"Yeah I promise okay and we can eat mashed potatoes that don't burn your mouth."

Richard is making a weird face at me.

"Okay," Noreen says like now she believes it. She pats my arm and is sitting up and looking a little more like the normal Mean Noreen. "Goodbye, Ronald."

27

LA QUE PUEDES TOCAR BACH

JO

"MIJITA," Mami whispers to me. "You're sleeping like the dead. Time to cook."

I shower and get dressed. Outside my window, I hear the plow trucks going by. Did it snow all night? When we got home from the Manor, there was almost five inches on the ground. Papi has probably been up for hours clearing snow off the trucks at the depot.

In the kitchen, Mami braids my hair and hums "Silent Night." The whole apartment smells like fresh masa and chile guajillos. I put on my apron and peel chicken off thigh bones, trying not to burn my fingers. Mami lays out the corn husks and dices potatoes that will go inside the tamales. I get a strainer from the pantry and put it over the big pot with the leftover chile sauce and chicken broth. Mami brings over the fresh masa and pushes it through the strainer, adding a little salt when she's done.

I whisk for twenty minutes with the heat on low until the masa looks like pudding. Mami checks it a few times and tells me to keep going. When it's finally ready, she plops a spoonful on each corn husk, and then I put on a clump of chicken and four diced potatoes. She inspects each one and then wraps it together like a perfect food present.

"I told Señora Reyes we'd bring another piñata tonight," Mami says. "Look for that Santa one when you go to La Rancherita."

I flip the tamales over and wrap each one the same way with parchment for cooking. "When is Tía coming?"

"Noon. We have to make the buñuelos and you know how she likes to talk. Speaking of talking: Do you know who was shoveling our walkway this morning before the sun was up?"

I say, "I'm going to help him after this."

"He would not take my money. That Ronaldo." Mami adds more masa to a tamale. "Es más bueno que el pan."

"He would say he's better than cheese."

Mami laughs. "That boy."

I wash dishes and wipe the counters. Mami stirs milk and cinnamon into a pot for the atole, my favorite Christmas drink.

"All this playing cello for the old people," Mami says. "Is it making you feel stronger?"

"I think so. I really wanted to get through my whole audition set."

"Next week you will show them."

The week after that, I'll show the Maple Hill string faculty.

I stir the atole in slow swirls. Yesterday, I felt good—better than I've ever felt onstage. The Serenity Room had calmed me down. And after the power went out, playing Christmas carols was just like playing for Harold and Eleanor—a key fitting into a lock. The cello was doing exactly what it was made to do.

I say, "Papi says my hands were made to play Bach. I can still do that if I don't get into Maple Hill."

"Sí, verdad."

"But if I get in, I can play Bach all day."

"This is also true." Mami pours each of us a small cup of atole. We lean against the counter and sip. "You have to make a choice, mijita. Are you going to hide in a practice room your whole life? Or will you take the stage? Me entiendes?"

I nod. Did I always know that? Or did Maple Hill make me see it? "But so much can go wrong up there."

"And what if your Carlos Prieto had said that?" Mami shakes her head. "No no no, mijita. You are being selfish."

"Selfish?"

"Sí—egoista."

"But I'm the one up there all alone," I say. "I take all the pressure of the song."

"Ciertamente—porque eres la que puedes tocar Bach."

I say, "A lot of people can play Bach."

"Is that so?" Mami cocks her head. "Was another cellist at the Manor last night who could play Christmas carols without music? Or for sick residents who can't go to dinner? No, mijita. There are others who can play—but only *you* can play for the people that *you* meet."

I want to argue—what does she know about performing? What does she know about stage fright?

But I remember how the beehive disappeared when I played for Eleanor and Harold. And the Serenity Room.

"I can't just stop being nervous," I say. "I do all the exercises Mr. Newsum gives me, but it's still scary—I hate it."

Mami hugs me. "Maybe it will never go away completely, quién sabe . . . but you have a *gift*. You need to share it."

In my room, I put on snow clothes. My cello case leans against the wall in the corner. Is Mami right? Do I *have* to play just because I *can*? How is that fair? I could never play again—I could be Esther. I could quit, and people would still hear the cello.

But not Eleanor and Harold—not the other residents.

I hate being scared about doing something I love.

Mami's response?

Do it anyway.

"*Hey!*" Ronny yells to me.

I pull down my winter hat and squint in the bright sunlight. Snow covers everything—almost. All the walkways leading up to the doors on our building are cleared.

I yell back, "*Did you do all that?*"

"*Haha yeah!*"

I trudge over to him at the next building. "What time did you get up?"

"Oh man real early." He digs into the snow and launches a pile off to the side. "Wow so many people emailed me last night and then when I was out doing it other people would come out and ask me to do theirs and look at this. Ha I was worried like maybe they'd change their minds if the snowblower guys came over but no way." He pulls out his wallet and shows me the money.

"How much?" I ask.

"Eighty bucks." He laughs hard and says it again. "Jo, *eighty bucks*. And I'm only on the second building."

I dig with him. "That's amazing."

"Yeah it's really wet snow and so people are all telling me it will save their backs ha which is pretty funny because I'm doing this basically because of a bad back situation."

My arms burn after twenty minutes. The snow is *very* heavy—like shoveling sand. Ronny attacks it, giant piles disappearing with each swipe. Every time I look over, I see showers of snow falling all around him.

"Now don't go having a heart attack on my doorstep," Loretta calls over to us. She watches from her stoop, wrapped in a big blanket. "Ambulance would never get to you in time, not on these roads."

"Ha yeah," Ronny says. "But I gotta get to the next building before the snowblowers come."

"You should drink some water."

"I been eating a lot of snow."

I say, "I need a break."

Loretta brings out cookies and water bottles for us. Ronny drinks his in one long swig and stacks his cookies like a sandwich. "Is your mom making her famous cookies for tonight?"

"Yeah."

"Oh man."

"I thought I had some hot chocolate for you, but I'm all out," Loretta tells us.

I say, "I can pick some up for you when I go to the store later."

"Oh, that would be lovely." She goes back inside and comes out with a five-dollar bill. "Keep the change."

"Ha Jo's Home Delivery Service," Ronny says.

A little white car with a plastic Domino's sign on the roof drives very slowly past us. The driver hits the brakes and hops out with a pizza carrier. He walks down the path Ronny and I just shoveled, and right up to the door of a woman, who pays him.

"You guys shovel this?" he asks us on his way back.

"Yeah," Ronny says.

"Nice job."

"Thanks."

"No—thank you."

"Ha yeah thank us," Ronny says.

I watch him drive away, and then look at the door he just delivered the pizza to.

I say, "Ronny."

"Present."

"Ronny."

He cranes his neck to look at me. Instead, he sees the delivery man stop at another apartment door.

"Oh man," he whispers. *"Jo's Home Delivery Service."*

28

RONNY AND JO'S HOME & DELIVERY SERVICE

RONNY

"THAT'S a lot of water," Glenn at the Foodmart counter says.

"Yeah people love water," I say.

"How many milks?"

"Uh six." I'm counting them again. "No seven."

"Bread?"

"Twelve."

"Hot Pockets."

"Twenty."

"Twenty-two," Jo says. She puts two more in the cart and is checking her list. "And five Snickers bars."

Glenn is adding it all up and oh man. "What's all this for?"

"Ronny and Jo's Home and Delivery Service," I say. "I'm Ronny and this is the genius, Jo Ramos."

"Home delivery?"

"Home *and* delivery," I say and I'm counting the money and paying him. "Like we take stuff to your house and also we're doing snow stuff now."

"You should make the name shorter," he says. "Easier for

people to remember. Maybe RJ's Home Service. Or just R and J Services."

"Ha yeah maybe," I say.

We go to the Mexican food store place next to Zoe's Fellowship and Jo is getting a piñata for the Christmas party tonight. Now we're at the Dollar Store for some other stuff and Loretta's hot cholate and oh man the cart is pretty full so Jo is pulling it by the front and I'm pushing. We drop off the cold stuff first and now we're doing the water and everything else. People are so happy and keep saying how great this is and Jo gives them my email in case they need more help later or if it snows again.

"Probably I could eat a hundred tamales right now," I say.

"Probably we should go eat some at your house and count the money."

"My aunt's here and they're making buñuelos. If we go back they'll make us babysit the twins."

"Oh man buñuelos," I say. "We can eat them too."

Jo is going right past her door to mine. "We will be stuck there. Trust me."

I lock the cart around back and we go in and now I'm making peanut butter and Fluff sandwiches. Bianca is like an inch in front of the TV watching an animal show with my dad and I make them one too.

"How is it out there, bud?" he says.

"Crazy," I say.

"A lot of business?"

"Oh man yeah."

We go to my room and I'm dumping all the money on Bianca's bed and counting it.

"Come on, guess," I say.

"Nine hundred dollars."

"Ha come on."

Jo is eating her sandwich and the Fluff is stretching way out. "A hundred."

"Nope," I say and I'm laughing so hard because *come on this is amazing.*

"How much?"

"A hundred and *eighty-five dollars.*"

"What?"

"Hahaha," I say and now I'm counting again because math is hard. I'm getting the other money from last week too and Jo is adding it all up on her phone. "Okay so that's two hundred and ten bucks plus the Manor money so that's seven hundred and ten dollars *oh man.* Minus that from FINAL NOTICE—"

"One hundred and sixty-eight dollars," Jo says. Her smile is real big and she can't believe it either. "We should check your email."

We do and there's like five more people who want stuff or snow shoveled. "Oh man but my arms are like dead and you have to help your mom."

"Call Mason," Jo says. "He can come over and help you until the party."

"Okay right."

"Hey—you should invite him. Esther is coming this year."

I pack up all the money and now I'm putting it under my top bunk mattress so nosy Bianca doesn't find it. "Okay."

"Weren't you best friends? That's what Esther said."

"I mean yeah but that was like in fifth grade before we moved here," I say but now I'm thinking about the Halloween horse in his garage and ha that was so funny when we did that. Probably that would be amazing to do again but do we still fit in it?

"You don't have to stop being best friends with someone just because you move." Jo is putting her coat back on and now she's giving me her phone. "Ask him to help shovel and invite him to the posada party."

"Okay," I say and now I'm texting him.

Mason this is Ronny on Jo's phone and no we're not going out ha gross. So I need help shoveling can you come over???? Yeah and Jo's family has a big Christmas party and it's tonight and you should come too.

I give her the phone back and it's buzzing already.

"He's coming over now to shovel," Jo says. "And to the party."

Jo goes back home and I get my shovel. Probably back problems are in my DNA because mine is killing me. Stuff hurts everywhere and I'm drinking all the extra water Loretta put outside for us. Now I see Mason coming at me with this really long shovel that has big handles and a wheel?

"Whoa what is that?" I say.

"I made it." He rams it into the snow and now he's lifting it up and wheels it way above the pile like a tractor bucket. "I call it the Snow Destroyer."

"Oh man that is so awesome."

"The driveways in my neighborhood are bigger so this helps." He does some more and mostly he's flicking up instead of throwing it with his arms which is way easier.

"How many did you do?" I say.

"Four, plus mine."

"Wow nice."

He's looking around. "Did you do all this?"

"Yeah pretty much everything you see me and Jo did. Probably I won't be able to move tomorrow."

Mason is digging and flinging snow all the way down the walkway. I do the smaller stuff by the doors and then we're done, two people in like five minutes. I knock on the doors and they're paying me and now we're going to the next building.

"It's cool over here," Mason says. "Everybody is close together and you have a playground."

"Ha yeah," I say but is he serious? These places are so small and have zero levels like my old house plus there's always trash and sometimes glass bottles on the playground.

Mason does mostly the whole part of the next walkway and I'm just taking a break watching. He's sweating big-time but we're done in like ten minutes and the lady is paying us ten bucks.

"Snow Destroyer is probably so happy destroying all this snow," I say and I'm giving him one of the five-dollar bills.

"Nah."

"Come on you did that all yourself."

He's shrugging. "You're saving up to get your Xbox fixed."

"Yeah," I say and is Mason the actual best friend ever?

There's this big rumble and now I'm seeing a red tow truck going real slow between all the parked cars. The big beard guy has his window down and his big stupid arm hanging out the window where it says *Vince's Towing*. He's dragging a black car behind him which is crazy because who takes people's stuff after a giant storm?

I don't even know what's happening but I'm making a snowball and packing it real tight and I chuck it at his big stupid red tow truck as hard as I can. There's zero chance it hits anything but for real what's his problem?

But wait there's a big loud *smack* because the snowball hits him right in the face *I mean right in the face*. The truck is going to one side and he's grabbing the steering wheel and now I'm running down the walkway with my shovel scraping the ground.

"*Ronny!*" Mason says behind me. "*Dude!*"

I just keep running and running and then dive behind this big snow pile that the plow trucks made. Mason comes down beside me and keeps looking around for the guy.

"What the crap?" he says.

"I'm not saving up for my Xbox okay," I say and I'm breathing so hard. "I'm trying to save our car from that guy."

"What guy?"

"Vince the tow truck guy. It's called repossession and he takes people's cars if they don't pay the bank for it like every month. That's us okay because my dad's back got hurt and he can't work and we got this FINAL NOTICE thing for the car. It's like nine hundred dollars we have to pay the bank by January first or Vince is gonna take it."

Mason is ducking real low. "Here he comes."

We get down and the tow goes right by us back to the light by the highway.

"Like how did that even hit him?" I say.

"It was a really good shot."

"Oh man do you think I hurt him? I really can't go to jail right now."

"That had to be the greatest snowball throw of all time," he says.

Now we're both laughing and Mason is showing me what the guy's face did when the snowball exploded. Probably it did hurt but so what? When you're a jerk face sometimes you get a snowball to your jerk face so too bad.

"How much more do you need?" Mason says.

"Like a hundred something. I mean it's crazy but it's going to happen I think."

Mason is getting something from his pocket. It's a couple twenty-dollar bills and is he giving them to me? "That's eighty from the ones in my neighborhood."

I'm looking at it and oh man this is like a two-person horse costume but with snow shoveling. But way more actually because he fixed the cart and brought the Snow Destroyer and now he's destroying FINAL NOTICE with all his money. It's like he never took the horse thing off and was waiting for me to get back in. "Whoa thanks."

"Sure."

I put it in my wallet and we're sitting there eating snow for a little. "My room is real small and Bianca sleeps in there with me."

"In the same bed?"

"Come on gross no," I say. "It's a bunk bed but she does always wake me up with her weird dreams."

"Huh."

"Yeah and apparently I have nightmares and yell NO like something bad is happening which makes sense because Vince is out to get me," I say. "Yeah and my dad is always doing his stretches for his back and it's super loud and the living room has a TV but Bianca is usually watching bug shows on it and yeah my Xbox is actually broken. So I never had you come over because of all that and I mean Jo lives here so she doesn't care. Her room is just like mine so she's used to it and we're not going out okay?"

"I get it," Mason says. "It's okay."

We eat some more snow and I'm trying to hit this sign with a snowball but keep missing.

"What's this party like?" Mason says. "Do I have to dress up?"

"Ha no," I say. "Just come ready to sing and eat a lot and also smash piñatas."

"I thought those were for birthday parties."

"Yeah it's Jesus' birthday but also Jo's family has piñatas at pretty much every party."

"That's cool," Mason says. "I never hit one before."

"No come on."

"They always made me go last because I was the biggest. It was always broken already." He's smiling real big now. "I bet I could get the candy out in one swing if I went first."

"You totally would because you have huge Snow Destroyer muscles," I say and right when I get home I'm going to tell Jo to let Mason go first because in the history of two-person horses he's the best other person.

29

NO MAS BUÑUELOS

JO

ESTHER'S mom drops her off right as we all walk outside.

"Sorry I'm late," Esther says. She hugs a tinfoil dish that smells like honey and nuts. "The roads are still bad."

"Rosa," Mami calls out. "The Russos are here. Light the candles."

Tía Rosa gives Ronny's family and Mason a candle, and then she lights them. Papi tunes his guitar. A gust of wind blows icy air right through my coat.

"Íjole," Tía Rosa says. "We're going to freeze to death before we can get Baby Jesus to the inn."

Papi starts playing and my twin cousins, Maria and Victoria, run ahead with their candles. They're supposed to be Mary and Joseph, but they won't let Tía Rosa dress them up anymore. We sing "Noche de paz" in English first, because everyone knows "Silent Night." After the second verse, we switch to Spanish. Ronny tries to keep up by repeating the sounds I make, but he's always a second behind. By the end of the song, we're at the Reyes' apartment building.

Maria knocks on the door. "We need a place to stay," she says.

A man Papi's age sticks his head out. He pretends to be annoyed. "I'm sorry, we have no room."

He shuts the door, and Maria giggles. Victoria knocks this time, but again Señor Reyes says, "I'm sorry, we have no room. Go. *Away.*"

Papi knocks, and then he and Mami sing the posada song—the story of Mary and Joseph looking for a place to have Baby Jesus. After Papi's verse, Señor Reyes flings the door open. He wears his own guitar, and everyone cheers. He sings a verse back to us—how there really is no room, and then we sing again. Back and forth we go, until they let us inside and we all sing about the angels and shepherds and Jesus being born.

"Josefina." Señora Reyes hugs me. "How are you?"

"Good."

"I hear many things from your mami. Many things." She winks. "La musica? Your cello? New school? I am so proud of you."

I pile food on my plate and sit with Esther on the living room floor by the Christmas tree. I devour two of Señora Reyes's empanadas and wash them down with soda. In the kitchen, Ronny tells Señor Reyes the story of his first cart crash—lots of hand motions. Next to him, Mason laughs. Food flies from his mouth.

"I thought about it more," Esther says. "I *do* want you to get into Maple Hill."

"Oh—thanks."

She eye rolls. "You know what I mean."

"You're not quitting?" I ask.

"Oh, I'm still quitting." Esther takes a bite of rice. "*Actually, I realized that you leaving made me want to quit even more.*"

I stare at her. "What?"

"Remember when you 'let me' do the solo last spring?"

"Yes."

"I wasn't really that nervous. Okay, maybe a little, but not much." She shakes her head. "But then you were 'sick' for the string competition at Dorney Park."

"I was actually sick," I say.

"I know, I know." She sighs. "It was just me, and everything was . . . different. I had to be *you*."

I say, "You're just as good as me."

"Says Bach to nobody."

"You used to be first chair," I say. "You can do it again."

"I know I *can*." Esther shrugs. "I just don't want to. All the practice time and pressure to be the section leader."

"You want to play drums."

She smiles. "Yeah."

I say, "When will you tell your parents?"

"After the winter concert, I guess." Esther puts her plate down. She pulls her knees up and hugs them. "I'm actually more worried about telling Mr. Newsum. I don't want him to be mad."

"I'll go with you," I say. "He can be mad at both of us for leaving."

Esther leans her head on my shoulder. "Okay."

We get mugs of fruity ponche and stacks of buñuelos. Papi and I sing "El niño del tambor" and Señor Reyes drums along on his djembe decorated with rainbow beads. After that, Señora Reyes leads us in all the Christmas favorites until Mami brings out the piñatas. The twins whack at the biggest one—a rainbow star with seven silver points. It holds, so Esther helps break it open with a few hits. She passes the stick to Ronny, but he gives it to Mason.

"*Snow Destroyer is coming for you, Santa!*" Ronny yells.

Mason slams the stick down into the piñata—*WHAMP.* Santa's head explodes, and then the whole piñata falls to the ground. Ronny screams *Wahhhh*, and then grabs Mason by the shoulder. They celebrate—this seems like the greatest thing that has ever happened. The twins jump on Santa and punch his legs until the rest of the candy falls out.

The adults want to sing more, so the six of us go into the spare bedroom. The twins flip through channels on the little TV until they find *Mickey's Christmas Carol.* Señora Reyes brings in a plate of buñuelos, but only Ronny eats them— the rest of us are stuffed.

"I wonder if you could eat them all," Mason says.

Ronny looks at the stack. "Probably yeah."

"No," I say. "There's too many."

Esther counts them. "Twenty-three."

"I'll probably need some milk," Ronny says.

"No milk," Mason says. "Just buñuelos."

"Haha great sign," Ronny says. "No milk just buñuelos."

"You're stalling," Esther says. "Eat up."

"Come on what if other people want them?"

I say, "She brought them in here because we have so many."

Ronny stands up and does jumping jacks. "Okay if I start choking does anyone know that move where you like hug me and the stuff comes flying out?"

"*Buñuelos!*" we all chant. "*Buñuelos!*"

He starts fast—three bites per cookie. Then he slows down, and we make him eat one every time the movie goes to commercial. Ronny lies on the ground to take a break. Mason puts one in Ronny's mouth and moves his jaw up and down.

"No más," Ronny says. "No más buñuelos."

I say, "There's only two more."

"Come on I can't."

"You're so close," Esther says.

"Is this how you want to be remembered?" Mason asks. "The kid who *almost* ate a whole plate of buñuelos?"

"Oh man fine." Ronny grabs one off the plate and crams it in his mouth.

"One more, *one more*," Mason chants.

Ronny picks up the last one. He moves it to his mouth very slowly. Esther drum rolls on the coffee table, and I boo when Ronny stops to burp.

Finally, he breaks it in half and shoves both pieces in with his whole hand.

"Why is his face red?" Esther asks.

"Uh-oh," Mason says.

Ronny coughs—crumbs go everywhere. He shakes his head and coughs again.

"He's gonna barf," Esther says. "Back up."

"Bathroom," I say. "Don't barf in here."

Ronny's face is completely red now. Is he laughing?

"He's choking," Mason says. He hugs Ronny from behind and lifts him up. "Need to clear the airway."

"Are you choking?" I ask. Ronny shakes his head.

"Hide," Esther says. "It's really hard to get the smell of barf out of clothes."

Ronny's feet kick in the air. He tries to break Mason's grip—too strong.

He spits out the whole mouthful.

"It was a burp!" Ronny yells, and we all laugh with him. *"Come on, it was a burp."*

30

MEAN NOREEN ISN'T THAT MEAN

RONNY

"PROBABLY it was a world record," I say and drink a big gulp of juice. Jean, Jeanie, and Carl are all leaning in real close to hear my amazing story. "I should call those people who run that stuff and tell them. I mean there was witnesses and everything."

"What kind of cookie was it?" Jeanie says.

"Buñuelos."

"Boon-yellows," Jean says and she's almost doing it like Jo says it.

"Boon-YOU-eh-lohs and it probably means 'best cookie you'll ever have.'"

"I haven't had a real cookie in years," Carl says. He's eating the sugar-free pudding stuff. "Can you sneak some in for us?"

"Ha but really you guys should get some piñatas for your holiday party," I say. "Like we can fill it with sugar-free candy or something but pretty much nothing beats smashing that thing until stuff comes out."

"Our ham was *spoiled* last year, remember?" Jean says. "For three months, Noreen told everyone it gave her food poisoning. I thought the kitchen staff really was going to poison her."

"Ha come on," I say and I'm looking back at her table but nope she's not there.

"She won't leave her room," Jeanie says. "Poor thing. That power outage brought back some bad memories."

"Yeah what even happened last year?"

"Terrible," Carl says. "There was an ice storm before Christmas, and a truck hit the telephone pole right on the main road here. Blackout, just like that. Almost the whole day."

Jeanie and Jean are looking really scared with big eyes. "The generators failed," Jeanie says.

"If they ever *worked*," Jean says.

"Oh, there was plenty of worry to go around," Carl says. "Our diabetes medication has to stay cold, you know. Lucky for us, Sarah is a quick study—she put them in coolers and set them in the snow." He points to his brain. "She's got it going on up there."

"Whoa that is smart," I say. "So Noreen is like scared of the dark?"

They all lean in real close so now I'm doing it too.

"They lost her," Carl says real quiet.

"What?"

"She moved to a new room the day before," Jeanie says. "But they didn't switch the name tags yet. So when the nurses checked rooms during the blackout, there was a . . . mix-up."

"Poor thing," Jean says. "She was alone for hours."

"Oh man," I say. "Yeah so that's why she was crying."

"Glad it was you she was holding on to instead of *Richard*," Jean says. "If I ever had a son like that, I'd cut him out of the will."

"Oh, because you're leaving behind so much money?" Jeanie says.

"I've got gold in here, sister." Jean is pointing to her teeth. "Do you even have any real ones left?"

I see Sarah talking to a kitchen worker so now I'm going over to her. "Hey maybe I could bring some dinner to Noreen," I say. "Probably she's not afraid of me anymore."

"I think that would be a great idea. She could use the company."

I get the tray and Sarah is telling me how to get there and now I'm walking down the hall toward Noreen's room. I knock real loud a couple times.

"Yes?"

"It's Ronny," I say. "I have food."

"Oh. Come in."

She's in one of those big recliner chairs reading a book with a blanket on her lap. She's looking at me but now she's reading again so I put the food on a little table next to her. The room is small but real nice with tons of books and probably most of the room is books.

"That's a lot of books," I say.

"I enjoy reading."

"Ha yeah."

She keeps reading and her oxygen tank is going *cushhh* every couple seconds.

"Man that snow was crazy," I say. "Like it was almost a foot of snow."

"Was it that much?"

"Oh yeah and real heavy. I was shoveling all day and could barely walk. Probably my shoulders are twice as big now."

She's putting her book down and looking at the food with her mean face.

"Ha want me to go heat it up?" I say.

"No," she says. "No, thank you."

"I mean I can really if you want."

She's shaking her head and is she sad? "I can't even taste it."

"Oh why not?"

"It's the medicine. I have to eat in order to take the pills, but the pills ruin my sense of taste."

"Oh man I'm sorry. Tasting is pretty much the whole thing."

"Indeed."

"What if I put a bunch of salt on it?" I say.

"Then it would taste like salt."

"Ha right. Hey wait Jo's mom makes this salsa that's amazing and I bet you can taste that. Like it's so good your taste buds will be like 'Whoa we're alive and it's a party in here!' But they might say 'fiesta' instead of 'party' because of Spanish."

Noreen is looking at me with her mean eyes but now she's

laughing? It's a lot of hissing and she's covering her mouth and wiping her eyes. "I was picturing my taste buds talking to each other in a new language," she says. "Oh, that's quite funny."

She eats a little and I'm looking at some of her books. "Man have you read all these?"

"I never put a book on my shelf that I haven't read."

"Whoa."

"Do you like to read?"

"Not really."

"Let me guess: You think it's *boring*."

"Ha yeah mostly," I say. "But I been working like crazy so maybe my life is a book and I'm reading the crap out of it."

"Books have been a great comfort to me all my life. Kept me company."

"Is this your family?" I say and I'm looking at this black-and-white picture of a guy and lady with a baby on her lap.

"It was."

"Oh man is that Richard? He's like a baby here."

"Eight months old, yes."

"And that's your—"

"He passed away," Noreen says real quiet. "But he wasn't around much longer after that picture was taken. He . . . left us and started a *new* family."

"Oh wow I'm sorry."

"That's very kind of you to say."

"They call you Mean Noreen but I don't think that's fair."

"Who calls me that?"

"People out there."

She's poking at her food but at least eating some. "Maybe that's fair. I can be a little short, sometimes."

"You told people I tried to kill you."

"I suppose I did overreact."

We sit for a while and it's just the sound of her *cushhh* oxygen tank.

"At the end of fifth grade, the bank took our house because we didn't pay the bills," I say. "Like they put one of those big orange signs on the window by the front door. Everybody could see it when they went by."

"Oh?"

"Yeah so we had to sell lots of our stuff and that was weird too because my mom did this big yard sale and all our neighbors bought our stuff for real cheap. Like isn't that weird?"

Noreen is nodding. "It does seem . . . discomforting."

"Yeah big-time. So our new house which isn't really a house, but like an apartment, wasn't ready yet but we had nowhere to go so the guy who owns them let us inside. But there wasn't any power or anything so it was just us in this weird house with no lights."

"Oh my. How troubling."

"Oh it was bad like real real bad and my sister Bianca had a night terror. She wakes up screaming and that wakes me up and I'm like where am I? So I'm screaming too and she's freaking out because she's like 'why are you in my room screaming?' but we shared a room now so it was confusing.

My mom comes in and she's freaking out and pretty much that was the worst night ever."

"Ronald." Noreen's eyes are all shiny and she's looking the opposite of mean right now. "Why are you sharing this story with me?"

"I guess because I know what it's like to be in the dark like when the power went out last year on you. That was probably the worst thing ever but I think maybe I know what it was like."

She's nodding real slow and wiping her eyes. "Yes, I think maybe you do."

"Yeah." I blink a couple times because *oh man* that first night in the Apartments was the worst night ever. "Okay I gotta go but maybe you can come back to The Lounge tomorrow night? Jo's doing her last concert thing and you gotta hear her. I think she's gonna make it through all the songs and it's gonna be amazing. Plus it will be my last time here so maybe we could hang out before I have to go."

"I'd like that very much," Noreen says real quiet. "Thank you, for bringing me dinner." She clears her throat a little. "And for staying with me, last week."

"Yeah sure."

"Did the lights ever come on?" she says. "At your apartment?"

"Yeah not for a whole day. We couldn't shower for school and my mom was trying to get rent money back because lots of food went bad."

"Just . . . awful."

"Yeah but then guess what?" I say and am I crying more?

"What?"

"I get on the bus and I don't know anybody okay, but this girl puts her giant cello in the aisle so I can sit with her. She said her mom was bringing us dinner that night because that's what people do when somebody moves next door." Oh man I'm wiping my eyes real hard because maybe that was the best day of my life right after the worst. "I'll bet you fifty buñuelos you can guess who that was."

31

THE FOOD BANK

JO

I ask Esther during fifth-period orchestra.

"Come to the Manor tonight and play," I say. "For the Christmas party."

"*Me?*"

"Yeah."

"I have math tutoring," she says. "Until four."

"The party starts at five."

"Violas," Mr. Newsum says. "You know how much I appreciate your sound. Oh, it is the sound of *heaven*." He leans on the music stand and stares at them. "But could you please, if it is not too much trouble, find a way—am I asking too much here?—to kindly *not* drag at measure twenty. Yes? Okay."

"They're going to rush it," Esther says.

We play the section again, and they rush it.

Mr. Newsum waves his arms for us to stop, and his hair falls over his face. "These are my hands. They direct music. Follow them and they will lead you to the promised land of syncopation."

"His hair is becoming a problem," Esther says. "He needs a ponytail."

The next time through, the violas play even faster.

"Just violas," Mr. Newsum says. "The rest of you, think musical thoughts or play chess on your phones."

Esther raises her hand. "Bathroom?"

I say, "Snack?"

Mr. Newsum waves at us to go. "Just sign out."

We go to the front office bathroom, and then get granola bars from the food pantry. Mrs. Ruth, the guidance office secretary, keeps it filled with leftover things from the county food bank.

"Why do you want me to come?" Esther asks.

"Because you're really good."

She raises one eyebrow. "Is this a trick so I won't quit?"

"No." I chew the granola bar. "You know how no one likes to listen to us during the concert preview in school?"

"Everybody hates it."

"Think of the opposite—times ten. At the Manor, cello *matters*. I don't know how to explain."

Esther picks out a chocolate chip from her granola bar and eats it. "What would I play?"

"Anything—you could do scales. They'll just love that you're there."

"You're still playing, right?"

I nod. "Last chance to perform all my audition pieces."

Esther shrugs. "I'll ask my mom. But I'm still quitting."

"Next year, you could do a drum solo."

Her mouth hangs open. "Do you think they'd let me?"

"We can ask Ms. Sarah tonight."

I hear a buzz, and then a loud *thunk*. A woman walks in the main entry doors.

It's Ronny's mom.

I wave, but Mrs. Ruth gets her attention first. Together, they wheel a big cart of boxed food outside to Ronny's mom's red Honda Civic. They load each one into the trunk.

"Jo," Esther says.

Ronny's mom hugs Mrs. Ruth, and then drives away. "Yeah," I say. My lungs feel cold.

"Jo." Esther looks around like someone might hear what she's about to say. "We used to pick up food like that when I was in elementary school. Before my dad and uncle started their restaurant. It's for people who are in trouble—*big* trouble."

"I didn't know." It's like my chest has a brain freeze. "I don't even know if Ronny knows."

"*Cellos!*" Mr. Newsum yells from down the hall. "*Let's goooooo!*"

We race back to the auditorium. I want to cry and scream at the same time.

I could sell my cello. I could get a job—maybe find another cart and help him deliver things.

Who cares about Maple Hill if Ronny doesn't have enough food?

"Oh my gosh," Esther pants. "Is he doing all that cart business to pay for food? He said it was to fix his Xbox."

"How nice of you to join us, ladies," Mr. Newsum says. "Shall we?"

Should I tell her? She already knows more than Ronny does.

We play the section all the way through—almost. "So close," Mr. Newsum says. "Right at the end there, violas. Just you, here we go."

"He's trying to save their car," I whisper to Esther. "They got a bill. They have to pay a lot of money in January or the bank will take it."

"How much?"

"Around nine hundred dollars."

"*NINE HUNDRED—?*"

I clamp my hand over her mouth. Mr. Newsum looks over to shush us. "He has almost all of it," I say quietly. "The Manor paid us to be there. He made the rest with his cart and snow business."

"Oh my gosh." Esther shakes her head. "That's . . . amazing."

"I don't think he wants anyone to know," I say. "Kind of like your *drums*."

Esther closes her lips, and zips them shut with her fingers.

32

VINCE THE CAR STEALER RUINS MY LIFE

RONNY

"MOM, what the crap?" I say because why is she picking us up after school?

"Need a ride?" She's in the Civic and waving at us to get in.

"What's wrong?" I say. "Did you get fired?"

She's laughing but really this isn't funny. "I always take off Christmas Eve-Eve."

"Oh right," I say because phew.

"Hi, Mrs. Russo," Jo says and she's getting in the back with her cello.

"Jo, we can put that in the trunk."

"It's okay."

I sit in the front and now we're driving behind a bunch of school buses that make like fifty stops.

"I'm going to come back later with Dad and Bianca for the final show," my mom says. "Wow—final show."

"It went by so fast," Jo says. "I feel like we just started going there."

"Yeah and who's gonna keep going there when we're

done?" I say because come on it won't be Richard. "Probably our school should get kids to go hang out there every week or something."

"I think it's really admirable what you two have been doing," my mom says. "They build all these nice homes for seniors, their kids pay all this money to put them there, and nobody goes to see them. It's terrible."

Oh man she's right and what if OPERATION FINAL NOTICE didn't happen? I wouldn't know Carl or the Jeans and maybe Mean Noreen would still be—

WHOMP goes the car like we hit a bomb.

We're sliding to one side and my mom is screaming real loud. She's not saying actual words but just like a really high scream that's making my ears ring. Jo's cello case bangs into the window and now it's flying the other way and *BAM* right into her head. My mom jams the brakes and we're sliding the other way so now she's turning the wheel we're going the first way *thunk thunk gushhhhhh* right into a big snow ditch.

My heart is going crazy but at least my mom stopped screaming.

"Ronny!" my mom says. "Stop screaming."

"What?"

"You're screaming."

"Oh man I am?" I say. "I thought it was you."

"Is everybody okay?" she says. "Jo—are you hurt? Ronny— look at me—are you okay?"

"Yeah yeah I'm good."

"Jo—Jo—are you okay?"

"Yes," Jo says but she's rubbing her head and sounds weird.

"Okay," my mom says and she's getting her phone out. "I'll call Triple A and they'll send someone to pull us out."

A couple cars go by and then a truck is pulling over. "You guys okay?" a guy says.

"Yes—thank you," my mom says. "Calling for some help now."

"Oh man is the car okay?" I say and it's like I'm floating and not really here. "What even was that?"

"I think the tire blew out," my mom says.

"That's bad," I say and I'm trying to think about how much money a tire costs.

My mom is calling AAA and now she's telling them where we are and what happened.

"Man that was crazy," I say. "Oh man, Jo that cello hit your brain cage are you okay?"

She keeps rubbing this one spot and moving her jaw up and down. "I feel dizzy."

"Not good," I say. "Mom, we have a head injury alert."

She hangs up and wow it's hard to get out. Pretty much we're halfway in the snow with the back of the car sticking onto the road. I have to climb out my mom's door because mine is blocked by the ditch and now I'm helping Jo sit on the snowbank. My mom is checking her eyes with the little light pen she uses for work.

"What day is it?" she asks.

Jo is blinking really fast. "Wednesday. Christmas Eve-Eve."

"Who am I?" I say. "What's my name?"

"Could be a mild concussion," my mom says. "Luckily you live next to a nurse who can check on you tonight."

"Oh man," I say because *the Manor party*. "Your big performance Jo oh man."

Jo is nodding but her eyes are all far away like she's looking way past me. "Esther will be there. She can play for them."

"The important thing here is that everyone is okay," my mom says and wow she's pretty calm for just crashing a car. "And we won't be stranded for long. Triple A said they had a guy right in the area."

My mom calls Jo's mom but no answer so she's leaving a message. I go look at the tire and man, it's totally flat and can you get them fixed for cheap? Probably I have enough time to make more FINAL NOTICE money but what about Jo's head? She can't get into Maple Hill if her brain cage is messed up for her audition.

"See," my mom says. "Help has arrived."

A big giant tow truck is coming down the hill and it's red with gold letters on the—

"NOOOOOO!" I say and I'm screaming so loud it hurts. "NO NO NO NO NOOOOOO!"

"Ronny—STOP!" my mom yells but oh man this is the end.

"He's gonna take it!"

"Take what?"

"He won't bring it back. He eats Nerds Blizzards in the winter!"

"What are you talking about—STOP YELLING!"

"CALL THE POLICE OR SOMETHING!" I'm making snowballs now and maybe I can do another miracle throw. Probably not but he can't take the car not now no way because we're so close.

"Ronny," Jo says and is she laying down on the snow? "Can you stop yelling? It really hurts my head."

And then wow blue and red lights are coming around the big bend and down behind the tow truck. My mom is going up to the big bearded *Vince's Towing* guy and they talk with the cop and then they're all looking at me.

"Oh man sorry," I say. "That's him Jo okay he's the guy who steals people's cars if they don't pay on time."

"He came to help," she says. "I told you—tow trucks help people too."

"Not this guy okay *no way.*"

The cop comes over and looks at the Civic and then an ambulance is here? Big Beard car stealer is backing his tow truck near us and hooking up the metal cross thing underneath. The paramedic guys are checking on Jo and talk medical stuff with my mom and now they're saying we can go home.

"We should call the Manor," Jo says. "Tell Ms. Sarah what happened so the residents know."

"Yeah but are you okay?" I say.

"She needs to rest," my mom says.

"You were gonna do great," I say. "Like I could like feel it Jo you were gonna play through the whole audition."

"Excuse me, ma'am?" Big Beard is coming over with a

clipboard and wow he's huge. "Was there a place you'd like me to tow it?"

"We usually use the garage by the movie theater," my mom says. "Across from the IHOP? I forget the name."

He scratches his beard and this close whoa I can see a big red patch on his face where my snowball got him. "Sam's Auto?"

"Yes, that's it."

"I know where it is," he says. "But I wouldn't take it there. I checked out your vehicle, didn't see any damage. Engine sounds fine. Kelly's Tire down by the bowling alley is your best bet to get a tire fixed."

"That's not on the bus line."

"You live in the Apartments, right?" he says and he's pointing at me now and I'm ready to take three steps back and run like the wind. "I seen this guy before at the Dairy Queen. I could drop you off on the way to Kelly's."

"That's very kind of you," my mom says. "We'd really appreciate it."

"Mom come on," I say but she's giving me this Mean Noreen face and I'm shutting up fast.

Big Beard and the cop talk more and we're climbing into the tow truck. My mom sits with Jo in the middle and puts her arm around her real tight. I'm smushed up against the door and everything smells like gasoline and doughnuts. Big Beard checks some stuff on the tow thing in the back and now he's getting in the driver seat. Probably he wishes he

could take it right to the bank people before he gets the special FINAL NOTICE signal.

"Thank you again," my mom says.

"No problem."

"Thanks," I say because she's giving me more Mean Noreen
eyes. "Vince."

"Bobby," he says. "Vince was my dad."

"Oh right."

He starts the truck and we're pulling out real slow and
going down the hill. He goes left on the highway and keeps
checking the mirrors and man this thing is loud. Now I'm
seeing this picture of a girl Bianca's age on the dashboard
thing wearing a Mickey Mouse hat. Big Beard is in the picture too and he's kissing her cheek.

"So you like Dairy Queen," I say.

"Not really," he says. "But my daughter does. I pick her
up one of them Blizzards once in a while. She likes the kind
with Nerds."

"Oh."

"Weird, right?"

"Yeah."

We go through a couple lights and he's turning into the
Apartments. Now he's at our building and my mom helps
Jo get out and keeps thanking Bobby a hundred times. Her
parents aren't home yet so I take her cello to our house but
forget my book bag and now I'm running back. Bobby gets it
and is handing it to me out the window.

"Yeah so thanks," I say. "For getting us out of that ditch and taking us home."

"Sure," he says. "I like the ones where nobody has to go to the hospital."

"It was me okay I threw it," I say because is his one eye still bloodshot from my snowball miracle throw? "Oh man I'm sorry I didn't mean to hit your face just your big stupid truck. It's not really stupid but you're always taking people's cars and it's the only one we have." I'm wiping my eyes and looking at the Civic way up high on his tow truck. "You gotta bring it back, we really need it okay or things are gonna be way worse. Like my mom already drives far for work and we almost have the money to take care of the FINAL NOTICE."

He's just watching me with his big giant beard face and is he mad? "I'm taking it right to Kelly's. I promise."

"Okay." I sniffle and my mom is yelling at me to come in. "Is tire stuff expensive?"

"Sometimes."

"Ronny!" my mom says. "Come on, bud."

I wave at Bobby and walk back through the snow.

"Hey kid," he says. "Nice shot."

33

THE NOCHEBUENA DISASTER

JO

I blink away the sleepers in my eyes.

Do I feel better?

I sit up very slowly. After a few seconds, my head pounds. I *should* feel better—I slept all night, lay on the couch all morning, and just took a nap. I can't use my phone because Mrs. Russo said my brain needs to rest. I can't look at a computer or TV either.

Papi pokes his head in my room. "Sleeping Beauty."

"Hi."

Mami pushes in behind him. "I'll tell Mrs. Russo you're up."

"You don't have to call her every time I wake up."

She calls anyway. Mrs. Russo, Ronny, and Bianca come over right away.

"Probably your cello should be punished," Ronny says. "It almost broke my face and now it's going after your head."

Mrs. Russo shines her penlight in my eyes. "Any nausea?"

"No."

"Headache still?"

I nod.

"How bad, one to ten."

"Seven."

"Down from an eight, that's good. How about your appetite?"

"She only ate a little breakfast," Papi says.

"If you're bored, I can read you books," Bianca tells me. "About bugs."

I am bored—but mostly scared.

Last night, the angry bees attacked. I woke up to get a drink, and they just took over.

How will I practice with this headache?

How will I get into Maple Hill if I can't practice?

What if Ronny's car needs more than just a new tire? How will he pay for that *and* the FINAL NOTICE bill?

"Rest is the best medicine here," Mrs. Russo tells me. "That's the way the brain works."

"I told Tía Rosa we're not going to the city for Nochebuena," Mami tells me. "We can go down next week when you're feeling better."

"Should we skip midnight Mass?" Papi asks Mrs. Russo. "Is it keeping her up too late?"

"I would see how she feels. But I wouldn't push it. Extra rest now will help her recover faster."

I say, "How long until I feel normal?"

She thinks about it. "Different for everyone. You just need to take it a day at a time."

"Can I play cello?"

"I don't see why not. Just watch that headache. If the music makes it worse, stop." She hugs me. "I should have made you put the cello in the trunk."

"She wouldn't have let you," Papi tells her. "She says it bounces around too much."

Bianca pats her stack of bug books. "If you want me to read one to you, have Ronny come get me."

"Thanks."

Mrs. Russo and Bianca leave, and I lie back down. My head feels better right away.

"Okay," Ronny says. He walks back and forth on the carpet. "Okay so this is bad but you have like ten days to get better. Probably you will be better in a couple days and then be ready for the audition."

I rub my temples. "Can they fix the tire?"

"Not sure because the Kelly's guy called my mom and said he'll do it after Christmas."

"I can't believe we missed the party at the Manor."

"Yeah I know." Ronny grabs his hair with both hands. "Oh man Noreen. I told her I'd be there but then I wasn't. What if she thinks I'm the new Richard?"

I say, "Get my phone in the desk and see if Esther texted me."

Ronny digs it out of the drawer. "*Where are you?*" he reads. "*I'm here. Sarah is asking where you are and I don't know. Should I play? This place smells weird. The decorations are nice. Where are you? Some lady is asking me where Ronny is—* Oh man that's Noreen."

"Call her," I say.

He dials and puts the phone on speaker. "I thought you died," Esther says.

"I'm okay."

"What happened?"

"Ronny here," Ronny says. "A tire exploded on my mom's car and probably we almost died."

He tells her the whole story.

"How was the concert?" I ask.

"It was really fun," Esther says. "They kept asking me to play another song. I think I performed for an hour. By the end I was just doing scales and they were *clapping*."

I'm so glad they got to hear someone play. "Thanks for going."

"Did you see Carl?" Ronny asks. "Probably he was dressed up in a tie or something."

"Oh yeah—he told me to say hi to you. Actually, most of the residents asked where you both were and if you were okay." Someone yells in the background. "I gotta go. Hope you feel better."

I say, "Bye."

"Oh wait—is your cello okay?"

At first, I don't understand what she said. "What?"

"Ronny said it bounced around the car."

"Yeah but it was in the case," Ronny says.

"Okay just checking."

She hangs up.

I stare at my cello case in the corner of the room.

I say, "Ronny."

"Yeah on it."

He lays the case down in front of my bed. It feels like each clasp takes him an hour to undo. When the lid finally opens, I watch his face as he looks up and down the cello.

"Is it okay?" I whisper.

He nods very slowly. "Yeah it's okay."

I get out of bed and look for myself. Very gently, I pick it up by the neck and have him hold it. I use the light on my phone to examine every inch. When I finish, I sit cross-legged on the ground in front of it and listen to my heart pound.

I say, "It's okay."

Creeaaaak.

I freeze.

Ronny moves the cello just a little—*creaaaaaaaaak.*

It sounds like the wooden floorboards at my tía's house.

"What was—" Ronny says.

I whisper, "Don't move."

Sunlight from the window hits the cello. I see . . . what do I see?

Maybe it's nothing—just a glare.

I blink three times.

A thin white line runs down the face of the lower bout.

"Oh no," I say.

34

MS. Q HAS NO LIFE, WHICH IS GOOD

RONNY

"WHY isn't Mr. Newsum calling us back?" I say. "Your mom said it was an emergency in her message."

Jo is on the floor looking at her broken cello and pretty much she's been doing that for two hours. "It's Christmas Eve."

"Right so maybe we go to where he lives?"

"How would we find out?" Jo says.

Oh man good point. "Okay maybe it's not really broken that bad."

"It's bad." Jo is playing a note and yeah it sounds weird. "Do you hear that buzzing? The more I play it, the worse it'll get. The vibrations make the crack bigger."

"Oh man," I say because her parents already called a music repair shop but everybody is closed for Christmas.

"His friend in New York fixes instruments," she says. "Last year his bass broke, and he took it up to the shop. It's the same place he found my cello."

"Okay so how long did it take?"

She's shaking her head and I'm staring at the cello crack because first her brain cage and now the cello?

"Oh man *Mason*," I say. "He can fix stuff."

"It's not a shopping cart," Jo says and is she mad at me? "You can't just add a few wheels and make it better."

"Okay but probably he has some crazy idea or something because his brain works like that. Remember the Snow Destroyer thing? I mean he made that."

Jo is just shaking her head but come on we have to do something so I call Mason on her phone and tell him what's happening.

"Coming over," he says.

He probably ran because he's at Jo's house in like five minutes and all sweating and breathing hard and he's got on nice pants and a sweater?

"Whoa," I say. "You're dressed up."

"We're going to church."

"When?"

"Soon."

"Thanks for coming," Jo says. "But I don't think you can help."

Mason has a magnifying glass and now he's looking at the cracked part real close. "It's cracked."

"Yeah but can you fix it?" I say.

"It's not a shopping cart," he says.

Jo is shaking her head.

"Your parents should call Mr. Newsum," Mason says.

"Yeah they did but he's not answering," I say.

"Email Ms. Q."

"Oh right wow why didn't we think of that?" I say and now I'm opening Jo's laptop.

DEAR MS. Q THIS IS RONNY FROM SCHOOL WITH A SERIOUS EMERGENCY. THE EMERGENCY IS JO'S CELLO BROKE AND WE CALLED MR. NEWSUM SO HE CAN HELP FIX IT BEFORE HER BIG AUDITION BUT IT'S CHRISTMAS EVE AND HE'S NOT ANSWERING LIKE ISN'T THAT CRAZY? CAN YOU HELP US OKAY THANKS. OKAY BYE OH AND MERRY CHRISTMAS.

I send it and me and Mason are just watching the inbox thing for a new message.

"She might not see it for a long time," Jo says.

"Yeah I mean who checks email on Christmas Eve—"

"She wrote back," Mason says.

"Whoa listen," I say. "She said she just told him and he's *calling your mom.*"

Mason's phone is buzzing and he's checking it. "My parents are here."

He leaves and we're barely done telling Jo's parents about Mr. Newsum when her mom's phone rings. Jo tells him the whole story and now I'm taking a bunch of pictures of the crack and emailing him.

"He said he would send them to his friend and ask about the repair," Jo says.

We go back to her room and are saying zero words. Now

Bianca is bringing over a bunch of ice packs and more bug books and I'm checking her email every five seconds but like an hour goes by and nothing.

"Mr. Newsum," her mom says and she's running in the room with her phone. She puts it on speaker and we're all standing around it.

"Okay so good news, bad news," Mr. Newsum says. "The good: My repair buddy can make room in his schedule. I'll drive it up on Monday, and he can have it done by the end of the week, no problem."

"Oh man that's amazing," I say. "Wow."

Jo is so close to the phone she's like eating it. "The bad news?"

"Did you drop it recently?" Mr. Newsum says. "Maybe carrying it from the orchestra closet to the stage?"

"No."

"Oh man," I say and the snowmen are starting to wrestle in my gut. Now I'm pointing at my cheek and am I floating? "Jo, my face remember?"

"That's right," Mr. Newsum says. "I forgot about that."

Jo is shaking her head but she's getting it. "We checked."

"A crack was probably made when Ronny hit his head on it," Mr. Newsum says and yeah I'm falling now because things are sort of feeling weird like there's zero gravity on earth. "It was likely *small*, and the car accident made it worse. The issue is the location. My repair guy thinks it might run through the bass bar on the inside of the cello face."

"What's that?" Jo's dad says.

"It's a piece of wood that runs top to bottom along the underside of the face. Mainly it distributes the sound across the instrument."

I'm sitting on the ground wishing maybe everyone would leave so I could lay down. Nobody else gets where this is going but I know exactly where and *oh man how is this happening?*

"It can be fixed," Mr. Newsum says. "But it's expensive."

No duh it's expensive and I bet I can guess how much. Like right now Jo's mom and dad are doing that real worried look because they don't have whatever money it's gonna take to fix it. Jo is seeing it too and now she's looking at me and yeah she totally gets it and is she gonna cry?

"How expensive?" Jo's mom says.

"Eight hundred," I say and I'm lying down in the doorway now and I don't even care because who cares? "Eight hundred and seventy-eight dollars and thirty-six cents probably."

"Close enough," Mr. Newsum says. "Nine hundred, and that's at a pretty good discount. It's a lot of money, but he's the best instrument surgeon I know."

Oh man I'm blinking real hard and my eyes keep filling up with water. Now I'm outside Jo's house and it's freezing and I'm going to my door and my parents are following and going *What's wrong* but I go to my room and get my wallet. Sarah has the big chunk but I have a ton here and it'll be enough.

"*Ronny!*" my parents say and now I'm back at Jo's front door with everyone behind her.

"No," she says and she's shaking her head but I'm holding the wallet out to her. She's crying too and just keeps saying *no no no*.

"Come on I broke it."

"Ronny—"

"*You have to take it*," I say. "Your mission is still going okay but mine's over."

She won't take it so I'm putting it on the ground by the door and going back to my house. My parents keep yelling *Ronny Ronny RONNY* but I'm running to my room. Now I'm on the top bunk screaming bad words into my pillow and crying because it's over oh man it's really all over.

35

THE WHOLE STORY

JO

WE don't go to midnight Mass.

Instead, I tell my parents everything—OPERATION FINAL NOTICE, start to finish.

They listen to the entire story, and hug me when I cry. It takes a long time, and when it's over my head hurts. They walk me to my bed, and Mami hums a song as I fall asleep.

"That boy," she whispers to Papi. "Más bueno que el pan."

I go to bed and dream about my audition. I play perfectly—but my cello falls apart during the last song. The wood cracks into eight hundred and seventy-eight tiny pieces.

I wake up at five thirty and get dressed. Ronny always said his mom gets up early for work, so I hope she's not sleeping in on Christmas. Quietly, I slip out my front door and knock on Ronny's.

Mrs. Russo answers.

"Hi," I say.

"Hey honey—are you feeling okay?"

"Yeah. Can we talk?"

I sit at their kitchen table. Mrs. Russo cracks a can of cinnamon buns and lays them out in a pan. In their living room, I see two stuffed Christmas stockings on the couch.

"One to ten?" she asks.

"Three. Not as bad as last night."

Mrs. Russo pours a cup of coffee and sits across from me. "Better already."

I look back at the hallway—toward Ronny and Bianca's room. "Did he say anything?"

She shakes her head. "He's been in his room since yesterday."

"He was trying to save your car," I blurt out.

Mrs. Russo freezes. She stares at me over her cup. "Our car?"

I nod.

"Why?"

"Final notice," I say. "He found it on your stack of bills, after Thanksgiving."

She turns her head very slowly toward an empty spot where the folder must have been. "He knows."

I say, "We called the bank—they told us what it meant. He's been trying to get enough money to pay it off so they don't repossess it."

Mrs. Russo puts one hand over her mouth. "The tow truck?"

"Yes. Ronny has seen him take away other people's cars here."

"So—Ronny thought—that's why he was yelling."

I nod again.

She puts her cup down on the table. "So working at the Manor? That was—"

"Yes."

"And his cart deliveries—the snow shoveling."

I say, "He only needed a little more money to pay the bill."

She leans forward. "He made *that much*?"

"He worked really hard. We all helped how we could."

In the back hallway, a door opens. Mr. Russo walks into the kitchen.

"Hey Jo," he says. "Merry Christmas."

"I think you should hear this," Mrs. Russo tells him.

I start from the beginning, and she helps me this time. When we're done, Ronny's dad has the same sad look.

"I thought he was saving up to get his Xbox fixed," he says very quietly.

I pull out Ronny's wallet from my coat pocket and lay it on the table. "I love playing cello more than anything in the world. But this is his—it's *yours*."

They stare at the wallet, and then look at each other. Mr. Russo reaches out and puts his hand on it.

He pushes it back across the table.

"The Ronny you just told us about, who spent the last month at the Manor and running around in the freezing cold to get this—if *he* gave it to you, then it's yours."

I say, "I can borrow Esther's cello for the audition. My parents said they will be able to pay for the repairs in a few months."

"I don't know much about music," he says. "But I don't think playing someone else's instrument for a big audition is a good idea."

Tears fall down my cheeks. "He worked so hard for this. All I did was give him my half of the Manor money—which I didn't want anyway. I only went there to get over my stage fright."

Mrs. Russo wipes her eyes. "This is a lot to find out."

For a few minutes, none of us talk. Mrs. Russo sniffles, and I rub my temples. Mr. Russo gets a cup of coffee and leans against the counter.

Finally, Bianca comes out of her room and stares at us. "What's going on?"

"Merry Christmas to you too," Mr. Russo says. He gives her a hug. "Thought you'd be up an hour ago."

"Where's Ronny?"

Mrs. Russo stands up. "What?"

"He's not in his bed."

Ronny's dad limps to the hallway. "*Ronny!*"

36

RONNY HAS LEFT THE BUILDING

RONNY

I push the cart real fast and I'm standing on the back and flying down the road between the Apartments and townhomes. It's cold but sort of feels good and a couple cars are honking at me but why aren't they at home for Christmas? I mean mine is going to be the worst one ever so I'm just staying out here. Last night I had this real bad dream and Bianca was telling me I was yelling so I never went back to sleep.

I zoom back up to the Foodmart and then zoom down again and maybe I can go all the way to my house without stopping this time. But like halfway down I hit this big rock and the cart is going to one side and *BOOM* I'm hitting the curb pretty hard. The handlebar hits my thigh and I go flying off into this big dirty snow pile.

"Hey," somebody says.

I look up and are you serious? It's the kid who lives in my old house and he's waving at me from his window which was my old window.

"Hey what," I say.

"Are you okay?"

"Yeah."

"I thought you were gonna do it that time," he says. "Go all the way to the bottom. That's what you were trying to do, right?"

"Yeah."

It's like before with Vince where I'm making the snowball and I don't even know what's going on but I got a good one in like five seconds. I'm throwing it so hard and it's hitting the side of the house right next to his window.

"*Hey!*" he says.

"Hey yourself house stealer," I say and I'm throwing another one but it's way short. The townhouses are pretty high up so you gotta throw it way harder. "How's it living in my room?"

"What?" He's ducking but I'm like not even close and they're falling on our old back deck near the grill. "Hey— stop. It's Christmas. Come on."

"Yeah it's Christmas and you're in my house so you *come on*," I say. "And your sister Charlotte needs to shut her big yap and find a new favorite color because *what even is Tahitian blue?*"

"You lived here?"

I make a really small snowball and I'm launching it *SMASH* right above his head. "Yeah and you better not have messed up the secret cave in the hall closet."

"What—a secret cave?"

I'm aiming another one but oh man my arm is so tired. "Like by the bathroom."

"The closet in the hall?"

"Yeah you have to jiggle the back panel thing and you can crawl through."

He goes away for a while and now he's coming back. "I found it. It's a perfect place to hide presents."

"Yeah my parents did that too."

"I was wondering where they hid my new Xbox."

I chuck the snowball and *BOOM* it's a bull's-eye so take that. The kid ducked but the whole screen is like bent and now I'm running away as fast as I can.

37

THE GIFT

JO

I hang up my phone.

"He's not at Mason's house," I tell them.

We're all in Ronny's living room—even my parents.

"Should we call the police?" Mami asks.

Mrs. Russo puts on her coat. "Not yet. We don't even know if he's actually missing."

"Maybe he went for a walk," Mr. Russo says. "Bianca—you didn't hear him get up?"

"No." Her face is white. "I'm sorry."

"It's okay," Mrs. Russo says. "It's all going to be okay."

I say, "Wait." I run outside, and check around back for the cart—gone. "The cart isn't there," I tell them. "We should check the bus stop."

"Good. Yes." Mrs. Russo nods. "Mark—you check with the neighbors. See if anyone saw *anything*."

"We will help," Papi says.

Everyone gets their coats, and we meet on the sidewalk outside.

Then we all stare.

A big red tow truck drives by very slowly—dragging the Russos' car. The truck stops, and then backs up into the empty spot right in front of us.

The big man with a beard climbs down and waves at us—Bobby. "Morning."

Mrs. Russo doesn't answer right away. "What—is something wrong?"

"Just the tire, like I thought," Bobby says. "No damage otherwise."

He bends down and unhooks the metal bar under the car. Mr. and Mrs. Russo walk over and stare at the new tire.

"I used to work down at Kelly's," Bobby says. "He owed me a few tires. Put this one on, good as she was before. No charge."

It's like Ronny's parents forgot how to talk.

"Thank you," his dad finally says. "Thank you so much."

Bobby gets back up in his truck. "Tell your son he owes me an extra-large Blizzard, extra Nerds. He'll understand. Merry Christmas."

He drives away. Ronny's parents touch the car like they are in a dream.

I say, "OPERATION FIND RONNY needs to start."

Mrs. Russo, Bianca, and I sprint to the bus stop. My head pounds, but the freezing air helps blast some of the pain away.

"I see somebody," Bianca yells.

I do too—but it's not Ronny.

"*Hey,*" Mason calls to us. He must have run over right after I called. "I thought maybe he'd be here."

I say, "Let's check the stores."

We run over to the shops and start with the laundromat. Mason yells *Ronny,* but the sound dies out in the cold wind. I go to Zoe's Fellowship and peek in the windows—a small church service, but no Ronny.

"Jo," Mrs. Russo pants. "Where else would he go?"

I close my eyes. The pain feels worse again—I can't think. Then I say, "Foodmart."

38

IT'S THE SEASON OF GIVING OKAY

RONNY

"LIKE why are you guys even open?" I say.

"People still need gas," Glenn says. He's got on this big green Christmas sweater with a red Santa hat. "Somebody has to be here."

"Yeah but it's Christmas."

"I'm Jewish."

"Oh right."

He's yawning really big. "Well my mom is Jewish, but my dad is Catholic. We do both."

"Ha nice."

"Are you delivering stuff to people on Christmas morning?"

"Uh yeah."

"Where's your cart?"

"Outside," I say and probably Mason needs to fix it but who cares anyway? No way I can make up all that money before FINAL NOTICE even if I had a hundred carts.

Glenn is yawning again. "Best part about working here is: They let me eat all the doughnuts I want."

"Whoa really?"

"Yeah part of the job. I got sick of it at first and didn't eat one for a while."

"Probably I'd eat a hundred."

"You can have one," he says. "It will be like I ate two."

He gets me one from the case with pink icing and sprinkles and now I'm eating the whole thing in three giant bites. "That's really good."

"They make them fresh every day."

"Man I wish I worked here."

"It's pretty boring," he says. "People aren't really that nice."

"Really?"

"They just want their food and gas and that's it."

"Yeah people are stupid," I say. "Okay I gotta go. Merry Christmas or Happy Hanukkah."

"Hanukkah was a few weeks ago," he says.

I go outside and man I wish Glenn gave me some water or chocolate milk to wash down that doughnut. There's some snow that looks clean near the big white townhome fence so I eat some of that. Probably I should go home now because everyone will be waking up and freaking out but no way because every time I think about *home* I want to throw more snowballs at the townhouses.

I keep going away from the Apartments and townhouses to the highway. Now I'm going past the bank and I throw a snowball at the big front door but probably that was dumb because they have cameras so I'm running away real fast. I go by the car wash place and now I'm at the candy store just cutting through the snow with the big cars and trucks zooming next to me. At the light where my school is there's a big fancy restaurant and a city bus stop so now I'm sitting on the bench freezing my butt off. I mean do buses even come on Christmas? Probably all the drivers have kids who want to open presents like a new Xbox.

But no wait there's this big engine sound and now a bus is coming up the highway. It's the regular one we ride home and it's slowing down right by me. The door opens and the lady is looking at me real weird. She's got the blue driver uniform and a big coat and a cool hat with ear flap things.

"Kid: What you doing out here?"

"I need a ride."

"On Christmas?"

"Yeah."

She's frowning at me real hard. "Where to?"

"Where can I go for zero money?"

"You don't have any money?"

"I gave it all away."

"That so?"

"Yeah it's the season of giving okay."

Now she's laughing a little. "I know you—what's your name?"

"Ronny."

"Ronny: You got about five seconds to tell me where you're

going, or I'm gonna call the police and tell them you look to be just about the worst runaway I've seen."

"No don't okay," I say.

"Then *where* you going? Home? *Grandma's?*"

"Ha yeah Grandma's," I say and my brain is spinning because my gram used to live right down the hill. "Like the Manor down the road is where I'm going okay. My gram lives there so that's why you're always seeing me on that bus."

"What's her name?"

"Noreen."

"Hmm," she says and does she believe me?

"I'll just walk okay I don't have any money."

"Get in," she says. "Like you said: It's the season of giving."

39

THE NEIGHBORS

JO

"HE was just here," Glenn tell us.

"When?" I ask. The Foodmart is warm, and I feel dizzy—too much running. But we can't stop. "How long ago?"

"An hour?"

"Did he say where he was going?"

Glenn thinks. "No. We just ate doughnuts and talked about working on Christmas. He said he was delivering stuff to people."

"The cart," Mrs. Russo says. "Did he have the cart with him?"

"He said it was outside."

The door dings, and Bianca walks in with Mason. "No cart," he says.

"How did he seem?" Mrs. Russo asks Glenn. "Was he upset?"

"Hmm. I don't think so, no. He had snow all over his gloves, like he'd been making a snowman."

I race outside and look down the road between the Apartments and the townhomes. Would he really just *run* away?

Then I see the cart—flipped over on the sidewalk by the tall white fence.

I yell, "*Over here!*" and we all run down. Mason stands it up and points at a broken piece of the frame.

"Now we're calling the police," Mrs. Russo whispers.

"Hi Bianca," a voice calls out.

We look up at the townhomes. A girl Bianca's age waves at us from the back deck. She has a remote control in her hand, and a robot plane buzzes above her head.

"Hi Charlotte," Bianca says.

"Merry Christmas."

"So you got the drone?"

"Yeah. It's hard to fly."

I ask, "Did you see a boy with this cart?"

"The snowball kid?"

"*Snowball* kid?" Mrs. Russo says.

Charlotte makes the drone land on the deck. "My brother was talking to a kid earlier. I looked out the window and saw him throwing snowballs at our house."

"Was his coat black?" Mrs. Russo asks.

"I don't remember."

I yell, "What time?"

The highest window on the townhouse opens. A woman shouts, "Excuse me—can I help you?"

"*We're looking for my son,*" Mrs. Russo calls back. "Your daughter said she saw him earlier this morning."

"Who?"

"RONALD . . . RUSSO," Mason yells.

The woman squints. "Russo?"

"Yes," I yell. "*Ronny Russo.*"

"That name sounds familiar."

"It likely does," Mrs. Russo says. "We used to live here."

The woman stares down at us. "In the development?"

Bianca laughs.

"No," Mrs. Russo says. "In your house."

"Oh. *Ohhhhh.*"

The window between the top floor and the deck opens. A boy that could be in our grade yells, "Your friend threw a bunch of snowballs at me. He broke the screen on my window."

"Did you see where he went?" I say.

He points up toward the Foodmart. "That way."

"When?"

"I don't know. After we did presents."

"Thank you," Mrs. Russo says. "And I'm sorry about the window. We'll fix it."

A white SUV pulls up beside us—*Esther.* She rolls down her window. "Did you find him?"

"No," I say. "But he went that way."

Her mom waves us all into the car.

40

MERRY CHRISTMAS TO ME AND NOREEN

RONNY

I get off at the Manor stop and I'm going in the sliding doors. There's like nobody in the hallway and even the front desk is empty because oh right it's Christmas. I'm going to the cafe and there's Sarah putting some red plants on the tables and does she ever take a break?

"Ronny?" she says. "What are you doing here?"

"Yeah I felt bad that I missed the concert thing so I came to say hi."

"On Christmas morning?"

"Yeah it's the season of giving come on."

She's fixing a couple plants so they're in the right spot on the tables. "Do your parents know you're here?"

I'm nodding but like not looking at her because there's a bunch of water right behind my eyeballs that is ready to come out.

"Okay," she says and now she's patting my back. "Do you want to wait here for Jean and Jeanie? They should be down soon for breakfast."

"No I gotta see Noreen is she awake?"

"Yes—actually, Monica rolled her down to the Serenity Room. Do you know where that is?"

"Yeah with the finches," I say and now I'm going to the finch room and Noreen is sitting in her wheelchair looking out the window. She's dressed up real nice like Carl with a white sweater and white blanket over her legs and one of those cool giant pins she always has on. Her oxygen machine is going *cushhh cushhh cushhh* and she's smiling like there is zero meanness in her.

"Hey," I say and I'm sitting in the big leather chair next to her. "Merry Christmas."

She's moving her head real slow to look at me. "Ronald," she says and now she's smiling this huge giant smile I've never seen before like ever. "I had a dream you might come see me."

"Ha yeah sorry I missed the concert. A tire exploded and my mom drove into a snowbank plus some other stuff."

"Yes, Sarah told us. Are you injured?"

"No but probably the car is messed up."

"Oh?"

"I mean it doesn't matter because OPERATION FINAL NOTICE is over."

"Perhaps I missed something: Operation . . . what did you say?"

Man I'm tired and so now I'm leaning way back in the recliner with my feet up and the finches are chirping right

240

by my face. "Okay so you know how Jo and I started coming here after Thanksgiving? Like she was doing it to get over stage fright for her big cello audition but I was doing it for the money."

"A video game . . . contraption," Noreen says.

"Yeah my Xbox. Right so I was also working like crazy after school and weekends to make money by helping people carry stuff to their apartments from the bus stop. And then I was shoveling snow and it was crazy how we were getting so close to eight hundred and seventy-eight dollars and thirty-six cents."

"Why that specific amount?"

"Okay so that's what the bank thing said that I found in my mom's giant binder of bills. It said FINAL NOTICE so we have to pay it by January first or they're gonna take the car."

"Oh my," she says. "That's quite alarming."

"And *oh man* we were so close it was crazy but then the car crashed and boom it's over." My eyes are all blurry and I'm covering them with my arm. "The Vince's Towing guy who's actually Bobby is gonna take the car next week because I had to give Jo all the money to get her cello fixed for the big audition because I really broke it with my face."

Noreen is holding my hand now and squeezing it real hard. "I'm so sorry."

"And there's a kid living in my room who got the brand-new Xbox that costs a bajillion dollars—"

"Ronald—"

"And we're never gonna get it all back," I say. "They're gonna take it and then how is my mom gonna get to work? Like all she does is work and she and my dad are always whisper-yelling about money at night *oh man* money is the *worst*. Like why is it even a thing?"

I'm crying like crazy but is Noreen laughing? Yeah she is and it's this real deep *huh-huh-huh* with her mouth wide-open and the oxygen machine *cushhhing* like crazy.

"Oh Ronald," she says. "You truly are the last and best hope for humanity."

"Come on what does that even mean?"

She pats my arm. "How about an *inherited lifetime annuity* —do you know what that is?"

I'm shaking my head because is she making these words up?

"When my husband left, he let me keep some of his money. And then when he passed away, he left me some more—out of guilt, I suspect."

"That's good," I say.

"Is it? I would have preferred to have been loved."

"Yeah he sounds like a big jerk face."

"That is an accurate assessment." She's playing with the blanket like Jo plays with her braid. "Richard says the bitterness spoiled me. I tried to make up for it, use all that *money* to make our lives more comfortable . . . it was a perfectly good life, you know. Nothing much to complain about." She's looking at me now and her eyes are real big and serious. "But in all those years, in all the people I've met, no one has ever treated me with the genuine kindness that seems so natural to you."

"Yeah but I almost killed you remember?"

She's doing that big *huh-huh-huh* laugh again and now I'm laughing too because it's so funny to see *Noreen* laughing hahaha. "You sat with me at dinner. You sat with me in the dark." She's grabbing my hand again. "You're sitting with me now, on Christmas. And I bet you don't even know what's about to happen next."

"Yeah probably I'm gonna be in super huge giant big trouble," I say. "Nobody knows where I went okay and that's not good. Like I didn't mean to run away but I just kept going farther and farther away from my house until the bus stop."

"I think your parents will understand."

"Ha I'm pretty sure I ruined their Christmas," I say but Noreen is shaking her head like it's no big deal.

"I think that when the day is over, it will be a Christmas that you never forget."

41

THE CHRISTMAS PARTY

JO

ESTHER'S mom drives past the movie theater—again.

I say, "He has no money. Why haven't we seen him walking?"

"Maybe he got a ride," Mason says.

"He would never get in a car with a stranger," Bianca says. "He would take three steps back and run like the wind."

Mrs. Russo's phone rings. "Mark—can you hear me? Anything? They're at the house? Okay, we'll be right home." She hangs up. "The police are at the apartment."

I lean my head against the window. The cold glass makes it hurt less.

Where are you, Ronny?

And why don't I know?

I'm his best friend—if I don't know, then nobody does.

Esther's mom turns the SUV around in the 7-11 parking lot. We drive back down the highway toward the Apartments. The traffic lights stay green—we'll be home in five minutes. I need time to think, even if it hurts my brain.

"This doesn't make sense," I say. "He has nowhere to go."

Finally, we get a red light right at the shopping center next to the Manor. I see the parking lot—almost empty. I hope their families visit today. Nobody should be alone on Christmas.

I sit up straight.

"Turn there," I say.

Mrs. Russo's phone rings again. "Hello? Yes—Sarah?"

Esther's mom parks, and I burst out of the SUV.

My head pounds with each step, but I run faster. The sliding doors open and I race into the lobby.

"Cafe," Ms. Sarah calls to me from the front desk.

I fly down the hallway and around the corner. Ronny sits at the round table in the back, his resident friends around him—Carl, Jeanie, Jean, and Noreen. Richard is there too. He laughs at something Ronny said.

I yell, "*Ronny!*"

He stands up. "Jo Ramos."

"We've been looking for you."

"Ha yeah Sarah's been calling my mom but getting voice mail."

"You need to get a phone," I say.

"Yeah probably that's a good idea."

I run over and hug him. Mason, Esther, and Bianca catch up and hug him too. "You scared everyone," I say.

"Yeah I didn't really mean to run away."

"*Ronny!*" his mom yells. She walks over and almost tackles him. "Are you okay?"

"Yeah I keep telling people I wasn't really running away—"

"It's okay," his mom says. She holds him tight, her hand on the back of his head. "It's okay. I'm going to call Dad. The police are at our house."

"Oh man really?"

"*Yes* really—that's what happens when a child disappears."

We bring more chairs around the big table. Ronny tells the whole story from when he left the apartment until he got to the Manor. It almost sounds funny—if I wasn't one of the people trying to find him. Other families show up, and soon the cafe sounds like a crowded restaurant. Mami and Papi drive over with all the food we were going to take down to Tía Rosa's—and a piñata. Ronny introduces all the residents to his parents, and then they tell stories of our time working here after school. The food and Tylenol from Nurse Monica make the pounding in my head go down.

"If I could interrupt this party for one moment," Ms. Sarah says after dessert. "Could I interest anyone in a game?"

We follow her to the Lounge, and see the piñata hanging from a coatrack. The residents take turns, and Mason gives them advice. Richard wheels Noreen up, and Ronny helps her give a few good whacks. On the last swing, candy flies out of the bottom and everyone cheers. She closes her eyes and laughs like she has been saving up her joy for a long time.

"*They have sugar okay people do not eat them!*" Ronny yells.

After we clean up the piñata, Ms. Sarah puts a black-and-white movie on the big-screen TV for the residents. Ronny, Mason, Esther, and I go to the Serenity Room to pick through the candy. I push the recliner all the way back and close my eyes. Everything is not all right—cracked cello, sore head, and a FINAL NOTICE the Russos can't pay.

But we found Ronny.

"Jo," he whispers. "You fell asleep."

I stretch. "What time is it?"

"Like two or something."

I open my eyes. Mason slumps on one end of the couch. Esther watches a video on her phone, curled up in the other recliner.

"Noreen wants to talk to me and you," Ronny says. "And our parents."

"Why?"

"I don't even know but is your head okay?"

"The nap helped."

"You gotta rest it okay," he says. "Probably you shouldn't run around outside looking for me again."

"I won't—if you don't run away again."

"Ha okay deal."

We walk back to the cafe to get our parents, and then follow Ronny to Noreen's room. She sits in a large chair surrounded by bookshelves. Richard adjusts the blanket on her lap and she smiles up at him.

"If I had all the money in the world, I would probably give it to your two children," Noreen tells our parents. "Or, I would burn it."

"Haha come on," Ronny laughs. "Don't do that."

"But I do not have all the money in the world. In fact, I don't have very much at all. The great majority of it went to my residence here, which lately is turning out to be the investment of a lifetime."

I look at Ronny.

He shrugs.

"Am I rambling?" Noreen asks.

"A little, Mom," Richard says.

He gives her a small booklet. Mami has one just like it—she uses it to pay rent.

A checkbook.

"Ronald," Noreen says. "Remind an old lady of that number you mentioned, for the car payment."

"A million dollars," Ronny says. I elbow him. "Haha no it was eight hundred—"

"Eight . . . hundred," Noreen repeats. She writes in the checkbook. "And?"

His mouth hangs open—now he gets it. "Seventy-eight dollars . . . and thirty-six cents."

She signs her name, and holds the check out to him.

"Probably this is a dream," he whispers. "If I grab it I'm gonna wake up."

Noreen nods for me to take it. I put it in Ronny's hand. "Not a dream."

"Oh man." He swallows. "*Oh man.*"

"Now," Noreen says to Ronny's parents. "If you're even thinking of saying something preposterous along the lines of 'Oh no, we can't possibly accept this,' then think again. You can, and you will, because—"

She stops. Her lips tremble, and she wipes her eyes. "These children . . . what they have done for me . . . for *all of* us. It has truly been a gift."

Ronny hugs her—hard, with both arms. His parents thank her over and over again.

"Ya viste, mijita?" Mami whispers to me. "Do you see?"

42

MAYBE IT'S OKAY

RONNY

"KNOCK knock," my mom says.

"Hey."

I'm reading this cool taco book that was in my stocking yesterday when we got home from the big Manor party. It's like the history of tacos and which kinds are the most famous in different Mexican cities. Pretty much it makes you want to eat tacos or go to Mexico or both.

"Dad thought you'd like it," she says and she's looking out my window. My dad and Bianca are watching some show in the living room with lots of singing. "I want to show you something."

"What?"

We go to her and my dad's room and she's pointing to our old house. "It didn't feel that tall when we lived there, did it?"

"Yeah and even bigger when you're trying to throw snowballs at it."

Now she's pushing the curtains to the side so we can see

better. "We lived there for five years, and you know something strange? I never saw the Apartments."

"Yeah but they're right here."

She's nodding. "I *noticed* them—I didn't *see* them. Not like I see our old house now."

Probably that kid in my room never looks down at me because he's got a giant TV instead. "I see it every day and I pretty much hate it. Do you know that Charlotte girl painted over the unicorn Dad made for Bianca?"

"Bianca told me."

"And she's getting drones for Christmas and probably they've got big cars like Esther's mom with the leather seats that heat up your butt."

My mom is putting her arm around me. "It's okay to be sad, buddy. It's okay to miss how things used to be."

"Yeah," I say and my throat is getting real tight. "Like is it ever gonna be the same? Are we gonna always live here?"

"Is here so bad? Your best friend twenty feet away? Neighbors who love us?" She's hugging me and I'm hugging her back so hard because it's like I'm falling off something really really high and I have to hold on to something or it's gonna hurt when I land. "Things don't have to be the same to be good."

I'm sniffling like crazy and probably get tons of snot on her shirt. "Is it gonna be okay with the car and everything?"

"The car is fine," she says. "But if we lose it, we'll figure it out."

"Yeah."

She's wiping tears off my face and crying some too. "I want you to meet some people—a little younger than your Manor friends. Fill up some of your free time now that you're done saving the elderly."

"Okay."

"I want Jo to come too," she says. "Think she'd be up for a practice performance?"

"Yeah because she never got to do her big show thing."

"Let's go ask her." My mom is kissing my forehead and hugging me. "First, we need to do a little damage control."

We go up the sidewalk to the Foodmart and then we're walking right into the townhome parking lot. The mailboxes are all in this one center part thing and a couple people are getting theirs. My dad used to do that but he wouldn't park and people would honk at him and he'd always say sorry but do it again anyway.

"It's so close but it's like real far," I say. "Like when I see it from my window it's like the moon."

"A million miles away," my mom says.

We go down a bunch of sidewalks and wow the lights and decorations are crazy. Way at the back we get to the row where our old house is and now we're going up the steps. Whoever is shoveling this probably should hire me because it's like a really small path and already icy. My mom is knocking on the door and it's weird because I'm waiting for my dad to answer but it's this other guy who is way shorter and bald.

"Hi," my mom says. "I'm Jane Russo—this is my son, Ronny. We . . . met yesterday?"

"Oh hi," he says.

His wife is here now and she sort of looks like my mom but with way longer hair. "Hi Jane—come on in."

"Oh that's okay," my mom says. "We just stopped by for a quick apology."

"Sorry I broke the screen," I say and the kid who lives in my room is looking down at me from way up the steps. "I don't even know how I did that because I don't play sports."

"It's okay," he says.

"Speaking of screens," my mom says. "We kept some extras in the attic. They're pretty easy to replace."

"I told you," the lady says and she's whacking her husband's arm. "That's great—thanks. To be honest, we never go up there."

"Yeah just make sure you walk on the beams," I say. "Because the rest is just that pink puffy stuff and you can go right through the ceiling."

"Good to know," the guy says.

"Please—come in," the lady says. "It's freezing."

"No—no," my mom says and now she's looking at me and I'm trying to move my legs but why aren't they working? "What do you say, bud?"

"You can play my new Xbox," the kid says. "If you want."

"Okay," I say and I'm walking in but it's like that floating feeling again. The lady shuts the door and we're taking off our boots and man it still smells kinda like our old house.

"Oh—you did it," my mom says. "The chair rail in the dining room. I always wanted to. It looks lovely."

The guy is sort of smiling and looking at the ground. "Turns out you should check to see where the sprinkler pipes are before shooting in a two-inch nail."

They all laugh and go into the kitchen and it's just me at the door.

"I'm Anthony," the kid says from way up the steps.

"Ronny," I say. "What grade are you?"

"Seventh. I go to St. Jude's," he says. "But I'll go to the regular high school after eighth grade because my school only goes up to that."

"Oh right."

He's waving at me to come up. "Come on."

I go real slow and man I forgot how skinny and steep the steps were. I walk by the bathroom and the secret cave closet and now his sister is waving at me from her Tahitian blue room which is wow really blue. I go in Anthony's room and he's giving me a controller and it's weird because he put the bed on the other side of the room to make room for his giant dresser and giant TV on top.

"Wow," I say because the window screen is all messed up. "Sorry."

"It's okay. Wait, did you break your cart?"

"Yeah pretty bad but my friend says he can fix it."

"Oh that stinks. I saw you with it all the time, down by the shops and at the bus stop."

"You can see that from here?"

"Yeah look."

I go over and man you can see all the apartment buildings going so far down by the highway. There's mine and there's Loretta's and probably I never really noticed them before either when I lived here.

"What were you doing with it?" he says. "The cart."

"I deliver stuff for people," I say. "It's like a business."

"Nice."

"Yeah it was pretty fun."

"And you were always with your sister or that other girl."

"Ha yeah my friend Jo Ramos," I say. "So like you've seen us out there a lot?"

"Yeah. You guys were always laughing."

"And crashing sometimes," I say and I'm sitting on his bed now which is way harder than my old one. "So how come you go to St. Jude's but your sister doesn't?"

"I don't know."

He gives me a controller and we're playing *Halo* for like ten minutes. He's probably a hundred times better than me. I see this *Halo* poster on the wall where my Nerf gun target was. It's huge and pretty cool and way better than a bunch of trophies.

"These kids were making fun of me," he says. "Where my sister goes. That's why I go to St. Jude's."

"Oh man."

My mom is yelling up the steps for me to go. It's weird being here but also I kind of want to stay a little more and not just to play Xbox. Like everything is different but it's also cool that now it's Anthony's room.

"Probably you'd like my friend Mason," I say. "He's the one who fixed my cart and probably will fix it again."

"Cool."

"Yeah I mean you could hang out with us if you want. He lives over in Fairways where the golf course is but it's only like ten minutes to walk there."

"Okay."

"Like if you see us zooming around just come out," I say and I'm giving him the controller back. "Yeah my friends aren't like those kids who were mean to you. Probably my friends would make a hundred snowballs and throw them at anybody who makes fun of you."

Anthony is smiling now real big. "Maybe you can come back and play Xbox."

"Yeah," I say. "Wow this TV is huge haha."

I go downstairs and we're saying goodbye to his parents and now we're walking away. I'm looking back at the house and man I miss it but not like before. It's still really nice and big but it's not my house anymore which is weird but maybe okay?

43

THE MEANING OF CELLO

JO

I step into the hospital elevator.

"Come on are you nervous?" Ronny asks me.

"A little," I say.

"Yeah but you're gonna do awesome."

Mrs. Russo presses a button for the third floor. "We're a little early, so you'll have some time to set up. You look lovely."

"Thank you." Esther let me borrow one of her black concert dresses—short-sleeved and lightweight.

She also let me borrow her cello.

"So is it weird playing hers or is it like a bike and you can ride them all?" Ronny says.

"It's a little weird." I practiced the last three days and most of today to get the feel of it. "But I like it—the sound is brighter than mine."

The elevator doors open, and Mrs. Russo leads us past a nurse's station. A *Happy New Year* banner stretches across a doorway ahead of us. At the end of the hallway, we walk into a large room with chairs, couches, and a TV—like the

Lounge, but bigger. I see the city through tall windows on the back wall.

"Whoa," Ronny says. "That's a lot of people."

A hundred, at least—most of them visitors, Mrs. Russo said. The New Year's Eve party is a hospital tradition. Patients from all over the building, and their families.

Mrs. Russo puts her arm around me. "That's your spot over there."

She guides me to a stool by the tall windows. In my stomach, the hive stirs.

"Remember," Mrs. Russo says. "You could play 'Twinkle, Twinkle, Little Star' and get a standing ovation here."

"I know."

"I'll get you some water."

I sit down and tune. The sound carries high up to the ceiling—a few people look over. Sweat covers my forehead. I slip on Esther's armband and wipe it off.

A woman walks over and watches me. She wears a rainbow headscarf and looks very thin. "I always wanted to play. But guitar seemed cooler at the time."

"I like the guitar."

"Is it hard?"

I nod. "But it's so fun."

She reaches out and touches the neck. "I always said I'd do it later. Next year—I'll learn next year."

"Anyone can learn," I say. "You just have to practice."

"I think I'll have to settle for listening." She plucks the

A string. *Deeeeeeee*. She plucks it again—louder. The sound lights up her face. "I'm Corinne. Thank you, for coming to play for us."

"You're welcome."

She walks away. Mrs. Russo comes back with a bottle of water. "All set?"

A few bees escape, and I squash them with a quick inhale. "Do you like working here?"

"Most of the time."

I say, "How . . . sick are they?"

"Some will get better; some we're not sure. Cancer is tricky that way."

I watch a man help Corinne to the couch. He sits beside her very close—his arm around her waist. A boy Bianca's age sits on the other side. "What about the woman I was just talking to?"

"Corinne?" Mrs. Russo smooths out a ruffle in my dress. "She's one of the tricky ones."

Most of the people have found a seat. I hear the room get quiet—they're watching me. Ronny walks up with a plate full of brownies and high-fives me.

"Ready?" Mrs. Russo asks me.

"Ready."

She gives me a long hug, and then turns to the audience.

"Hi everyone—friends of friends, family, people of far-away lands like the fifth floor. Happy New Year's Eve. Aren't these decorations incredible?" Everyone nods and claps.

"Tonight, my son's friend Josefina Ramos will be performing several cello pieces. I've been told clapping is appropriate after each one—Ronny, is that right?"

"That is correct," Ronny says. "But at the end of the song okay not like in the middle after a really cool part."

"Good, good. Okay, well, that's enough from me. I hope you enjoy the show—and happy New Year."

She walks away.

A few bees buzz around my stomach. *I am nervous. It is normal to be nervous.* I adjust the music on the stand—*Arioso*, prelude in D Minor, and then G.

All three audition songs.

All the way through.

My fingers find their starting positions. I lift the bow.

I count myself in:

One and

Two and

Ready and—

The hive explodes.

The bees have turned into giant hornets. They crash into my intestines—my whole stomach vibrates.

No.

This *can't* be happening. All the breathing and stretching and afternoons at the Manor—why hasn't anything changed? Why can't I get *over* this? I'm not hiding in a practice room—I am here to play *for* these people.

And then I see Corinne. She nods at me. *Play,* she mouths. *Please.*

Some will get better, Mrs. Russo said. *Some we're not sure.*

Why wouldn't you want other people to hear it too? Mr. Newsum asked me.

And Mami. *You are the one who can play Bach.*

I think of Eleanor and Harold. Carl, Jean, Jeanie—Noreen. Corinne.

In my head, I hear a melody—Schumann's *Three Fantasy Pieces.* My favorite one. It gets louder, and the hornets slow down. That warm wave rises and carries me off my feet. I pick up the stool and walk into the audience.

Ronny stares at me, and I smile back so wide, it hurts. I don't feel scared because *this isn't about me.* Yes, I am the one who can play Bach.

But it's the music that people love—that's why the cello matters.

I put the stool down near Corinne. "I want to play you the piece that made me fall in love with the cello."

44

BACH HAS A BIG GIANT HEAD

RONNY

"WHOA," I say. "That's a big sign."

Jo's mom drives real slow into the Maple Hill entrance and we go by this huge stone wall with a giant sign saying *MAPLE HILL CONSERVATORY*. Now we're driving down a big wide driveway with these huge trees going way up high on both sides. Jo looks fancy in the dress Esther gave her and doing stuff with her fingers on the seat like she's playing a song.

Her mom parks and now we're walking across the parking lot to the main office and this guy with white hair and a suit is waiting for us inside.

"Josefina, welcome," he says. "I'm Mr. Buckley, head of admissions. It's a pleasure to finally meet you."

"Thank you for having me," Jo says and she's shaking his hand. "The campus is beautiful."

"It is, especially in winter," he says and we're following him down a big hallway with tons of glass cases full of big shiny trophies. The guy is saying stuff about the classrooms and waving to teachers but oh man Jo is in her cello zone.

She told me the bees are still there sometimes but she has a new special power to crush them which means she is going to crush this audition.

"Here we are," Mr. Buckley says and now we're at the auditorium. It's way nicer than our school one with real tall ceilings and balconies and nice carpet floors. Way up on the stage is a piano and there's a couple teachers around in chairs probably talking about how awesome music is. Oh man there's an empty chair in front and I know that's for Jo.

"I deliver you to: the string faculty," the Buckley guy says. "We'll be at the cafeteria, just over there. They'll bring you down when the audition is finished."

Jo's mom hugs her and holds her face with both hands and says stuff in Spanish real quiet. Now she's going down the hallway with the Buckley guy and it's just me and Jo.

"You're gonna do awesome," I say. "Like what do these people even know about cello? Probably you could teach them come on."

Jo is hugging me. "Thanks for coming."

"Yeah I mean this got me out of school."

We high-five and one of the cello teachers is coming to get Jo. He closes the door but it goes real slow so I'm seeing her up the aisle to the stage and I hope she's crushing bees. Then it's just me staring at the door and a couple kids walk by wearing the same uniforms Jo will have next year.

I go to the cafeteria but it's weird with Jo's mom and the Buckley guy so now I'm going outside to this garden place with a bunch of walkways. It's shoveled real good and you can see they have brick instead of regular sidewalk because it's a fancy school.

I go around some bushes and there's this big giant statue but it's just a head. The guy has a wig on and he's making this real serious face and now I'm reading the words under him. It says *Johann Sebastian Bach: 1685–1750.*

There's room up on the cement thing next to his head so I'm climbing up. It's real quiet and there's kids on pathways going through the woods to other buildings. The big auditorium is up the hill and Jo is in there crushing it. She's gonna get in and be the next Carlos Prieto and not go to my school. Yeah it will be sad but I mean she's not moving like Ms. Q said and Mason is still there and Esther will eat with us probably. It's not the same without Jo but probably it's not the worst? I mean moving to the Apartments was the worst but then Jo was there so maybe not that bad actually.

I'm freezing my butt off and probably Jo's mom thinks I'm lost or ran away again so I should go back but now Jo is coming down the path.

"Oh man it's done," I say. "Like you did it. That was so fast."

"It felt like an hour."

"Was it good?"

"I think so," she says and she's getting up on the other side of Bach's head. "I did my best."

"Bees?"

"A little."

"Man did you see the uniforms?" I say. "Is it like red or brown?"

"I think it's maroon," she says.

"Ha I mean is that even a color?"

Jo is leaning her head on Bach's giant head and humming this song he probably wrote. "They have an ice cream machine in the cafeteria," she says. "The swirly kind with both flavors."

"Whoa really?"

"Yeah."

"Like chocolate and vanilla in one?"

"Let's go get some."

She counts to three and now we're jumping off Bach's head into a big pile of snow.

EPILOGUE

6 MONTHS LATER

RONNY

"OH man it's hot," I say.

Mason is way ahead of me pushing his cart with big piles of laundry bags in it. "I think it's the humidity."

"Like it's a million degrees."

We get to the shops and now we're taking a break in the shade. Mason gives me a bottle of this blue stuff that says *Sports Hydration TO THE MAX!* and I'm drinking the whole thing.

"My mom got them online," he says. "It's supposed to taste like Gatorade."

We keep going to the laundromat and we're pushing the carts inside. Mason said we had to get this thing organized because a couple weeks ago we gave Loretta's underwear to the wrong person so now we write everything down. The guy who owns the place said we could label the washers and dryers with numbers so Mason got this cool label maker and we did.

I put all the bags on top of the machines and I'm getting my notebook and writing down which one is where. Mason does the other side and we're putting them all in at the same time. Some people forget to separate colors and whites so I fix a couple and now Mason is measuring the detergent stuff.

"Symphony wants the fabric softener," Mason says.

"Oh right," I say and I'm grabbing some and putting it in the machines. "All good?"

"Good."

In the way back there's a change maker by the soda machine so we're sticking our bills in and getting quarters. We go to the washers and triple-check all the settings and now we're putting the coins in and starting them up.

"What time are they coming?" Mason says.

"Pretty soon I think because their thing starts at ten."

"How come she's doing it at Zoe's Fellowship and not school?"

"Jo wants it to be just for the Apartment kids," I say. "And like if their parents don't have a car they can walk to it. She asked the pastor guy and he said it was an awesome idea."

We get sodas and stand by this one big fan in the front so it's blasting our faces. There's no air-conditioning in here and people hate waiting for their wash so that's why we have so many orders.

"I think that's them," Mason says.

We run real fast across the parking lot to Zoe's Fellowship where this truck and little trailer are pulling up. Esther and

Jo come out of Zoe's and they're wearing these neon-green T-shirts that say *Warrington String Camp* with a picture of a cello. Bianca is inside already setting up name tags on a table.

"Ron-*eeeeeee*," Mr. Newsum says. "What's up, bud?"

"I'm sweating like crazy."

"Yeah, we better get these instruments out of the heat. Wouldn't want to get the *famous* Kennesaw orchestra director in *trouble* now would we? Not after he was kind enough to loan us these beauties."

Ms. Q gets out too and now we're all carrying the cases inside.

"So how's the laundry business?" Ms. Q no wait I mean Mrs. Newsum says.

"Yeah pretty gross at first," I say. "But then when we wash them it's not bad."

"Makes sense."

We put the stuff in the front where Jo and Esther are setting up all the music stands.

"Probably I'm gonna still call you Ms. Q," I say. "Like by accident but in my head you'll always be Ms. Q."

She's giving me a high five. "To always being Ms. Q."

JO

I put the girl's bow on the biggest string.

"This is C," I say. "Play it like me."

She watches, and then pulls the bow across hers. "Like that?"

"A little more pressure."

This time, the cello sings a deep note. Her eyes light up. "Wow."

"Try the next one up—that's the G. It should be easier because the string is thinner."

She plays the G, and then the D and A. I fix her grip on the bow, and then play a few notes on my cello. She goes back down to the C and pushes the bow back and forth, back and forth.

"It's hard," she says. "To make it sound good every time."

"It gets easier—if you practice. A lot."

"How long?"

"Depends on how much you love it."

She sets her bow back on the string. "Show me again."

When it's almost noon, Mr. Newsum calls everyone back together for a pitch exercise. We sing as he plays scales on the keyboard, and then parents begin to show up. Mrs. Newsum and Bianca do check-outs with each camper at the door, and then we wave goodbye as they walk home. Ronny and Mason come back to help us load the instruments into the trailer.

"Did you hear Simone, the girl I was playing with?" Esther asks me. "She's going to be *good*."

"May she have all of your pitch, and none of your sweating," Mr. Newsum says. He points at her. "Don't even think about recruiting her to your new percussion habits."

Bianca taps her clipboard. "Selena, the girl with glasses, said her brother will be coming tomorrow. She thinks he wants to try the violin."

"The more the merrier," Mrs. Newsum says. "We have plenty of them."

Mr. Newsum shuts the trailer and locks it. "Quite the camp you've got here, Jo-Jo Ma."

I say, "Thanks for asking the school to let us borrow these."

"Oh, I needed some convincing." He kisses Mrs. Newsum on the cheek. "But this is a compelling endeavor: the youth of America teaching strings to the youth of America. For free."

"Guys, are we going to Dairy Queen or what?" Ronny asks. "Me and Mason have like ten minutes before the dryers are done."

I check the main room one more time for any trash, and then let the church secretary know I'm leaving.

At Dairy Queen, Ronny reminds everyone to put their orders on his tab.

"Probably a lot of my money goes to ice cream," he tells Mrs. Newsum. "But come on that's a good use of money."

We sit by the window and eat. Bianca gets a brain freeze from eating her extra Nerds Blizzard too fast. When Mr. and Mrs. Newsum leave to take the instruments back to school, we walk next door to the laundromat.

"How many bags are you doing at a time?" I ask Ronny.

He checks his clipboard. "Fifteen this morning."

"Wow."

"Yeah it's crazy."

"We should get more detergent this weekend," Mason says. "Almost out."

Ronny writes that down.

When the loads are done, I push one of the carts for drop-off. Ronny marks off each apartment in his notebook as we put the bags by each door. Some of the people aren't home, so Mason emails them from his phone.

When all the deliveries are finished, we walk over to the playground. Mason plays basketball with Esther and Bianca. Ronny and I collapse in the shade.

"Isn't it weird that they're married?" Ronny asks me.

"It's cool." I played at their wedding last month. I did *not* drop my cello. "I'm glad they are."

"Yeah but she's always gonna be Ms. Q."

I sip the blue sports drink Mason gave us. "I didn't think so many kids would come to the camp."

"I mean we put the flyers on every door."

"Mr. Newsum said we can fill out special papers this fall to buy instruments—it's called a grant. The school district awards one each year to different groups."

"Whoa nice."

Esther shoots. The ball bounces off the rim so hard, it almost flies over the fence.

"So are you still mad?" Ronny asks me. "I mean come on that was so dumb you didn't get in."

That was *not* a good day. Actually, it was not a good month.

I say, "Sometimes it makes me angry. And sad."

"Probably they're regretting it big-time."

I shrug. "I did my best."

"Yeah and you've only been playing a couple years when those other cello nerds were doing it their whole lives."

The sun finds a way through the trees and shines on my face. "When I think about it too much, I just play more cello. That helps it go away."

Ronny and I join the game. Anthony, the boy who lives in Ronny's old room, walks over from the townhomes— everybody wants him on their team because he's taller. It's very hot, so we go back to Ronny's and watch a movie in the air-conditioning. He makes peanut butter and Fluff sandwiches, and we try not to get any on the couch. When the movie ends, Esther's mom picks her up and takes Mason and Anthony home too.

"Let's watch all the Star Wars movies in a row," Ronny says. "Come on we can do it."

"I have to practice for Friday."

"Oh right."

I walk to my apartment and change out of my sweaty T-shirt. After warming up, I get out the new piece I've been working on—*The Swan* by Camille Saint-Saëns, a French composer who lived a long time ago. The melody is slow and dramatic, which also makes it very hard. All the notes have continuous vibrato, so the shifting has to be just right. I can't *wait* to play it for the Manor residents.

I lift my bow, and count in.

One and

Two and

Ready and

Go.

AUTHOR'S NOTE

The Apartments, townhomes, and Mason's neighborhood with the public golf course are based on real places my students live. You can walk to each one in about ten minutes—less if you have a tricked-out shopping cart with pink Razor wheels. The physical closeness and experiential distance of these communities has always struck me, and I wanted to tell a story about the amazing kids who live there. They come into my room with unique burdens—financial instability, anxiety, parental pressure, and loneliness. Despite these, they somehow learn social studies. They amaze me.

I played a lot of cello while writing this book, most of it poorly. Like Jo, I experience pretty severe stage fright ever since a piano-recital-gone-wrong at age ten. I've never stopped playing music, but never fully shook the nerves. Jo's breakthrough was therefore cathartic, perhaps even prophetic for my own journey. *What is the point of music?* is a question worth asking, I think. If you listen to the pieces I've used in this story—especially the Bach suites—you might discover one possible answer: to be overwhelmed by the sheer magnitude of its beauty. To be robbed of any other reply than *wow*.

ACKNOWLEDGMENTS

Two insiders made this story real. The first is my friend and orchestra teacher, Pat. We spent many hours after school talking strings, Bach, and the competitive world of adolescent conservatories. Not only is he an accomplished bassist (that big giant cello thing), but he is incredibly kind. He gave me many lessons and lent me the cello that I played during this project. He served as the template for Mr. Newsum, and in return I agreed to give him zero money.

My cousin's wife, Victoria, graciously shared her immigrant experience on all things Mexican. Her linguistic and cultural insights added, brightened, changed, and fixed elements of Jo to make her authentic. Not only did Victoria read the manuscript, but she also weighed in on my many essay-long texts and emails before, during, and after the project's completion. I also recall an epic video of her three-year-old daughter beating the living daylights out of a piñata at a posada party. Should you ever find your own Christmas party boring, consider adding one to your activity list. Or five.

My wife, Kristy, has been telling me to write a dual POV

story for years. It was my hardest project so far, but I'm glad I did it. She also suggested I add more commas to Ronny's narration, which I mostly ignored. Probably her best skill is finding typos during late-night reading sessions on our family Kindle, which is so old, she has to use her phone to take pictures of her finger pointing to the error and then text them to me.

My agent, Lauren Galit, championed this project from start (a really broad and terrible idea three years ago) to finish (the sentence you're reading). She kept my book-life in order during a chaotic editing season, which pretty much boiled down to saying "relax" after I'd fired off a long email full of overdramatic writing woes. She should get a raise. I'll talk to my agent about it.

My editor, Michelle Lee, adopted this project after Dana Chidiac earned an amazing promotion elsewhere. Michelle played rapturous catch-up and brought clarity to the story so readers could get what I was getting at. Specifically, she helped me draw clear boundaries between Ronny and Jo in thought, speech pattern, and action. She also annoyingly kept putting commas into the Ronny chapters, which I promptly deleted, only to later find inserted again. Pretty much it became a hilarious game that neither of us was 100 percent joking about.

The team at Dial never makes it onto the book jacket, but they actually make the book happen. Witness their names and greatness: cover designer Tony Sahara and artist Rafael

Mayani, who absolutely nailed the themes and tension; Cerise Steel, whose interior design gave this a marvelous feel; Editorial Director Nancy Mercado, who has a special skill at sharpening chapter endings; and copy editor Regina Castillo, who really just freaking rocks. She's like a draft-reading vigilante who hunts down errors and delivers swift street justice, which in this metaphor is deleting, capitalizing, fact-checking, and highlighting repetitive words that would otherwise make me look silly. Also Kenny Young straight up slayed on later edit rounds. I demand a statue be built in his honor.

And my students, who inhabit my first and favorite world: the classroom. They teach me, challenge me (talking about you, third and sixth periods), and inspire me to write stories in their world. I love my job, and I love them. Most of them.